Dedalus Europe 2016
General Editor: Timothy Lane

The Interpreter

To Simona, Alessandro and Elisabetta

Diego Marani

THE
INTERPRETER

Translated by Judith Landry

Dedalus

This book has been published with the support of Ministero Affari Esteri Italiano and Arts Council England, London.

Supported using public funding by
ARTS COUNCIL ENGLAND

Published in the UK by Dedalus Limited,
24-26, St Judith's Lane, Sawtry, Cambs, PE28 5XE
email: info@dedalusbooks.com
www.dedalusbooks.com

ISBN printed book 978 1 910213 12 4
ISBN ebook 978 1 910213 19 3

Dedalus is distributed in the USA & Canada by SCB Distributors,
15608 South New Century Drive, Gardena, CA 90248
email: info@scbdistributors.com   web: www.scbdistributors.com

Dedalus is distributed in Australia by Peribo Pty Ltd.
58, Beaumont Road, Mount Kuring-gai, N.S.W. 2080
email: info@peribo.com.au

Publishing History
First published in Italy in 2004
First Dedalus edition in 2016

L'interprete © copyright Diego Marani 2004
Published by arrangement with Marco Vigevani Agenzia Letteraria
The Interpreter translation © copyright Judith Landry 2016

Printed in Finland by Bookwell
Typeset by Marie Lane

Diego Marani

Diego Marani was born in Ferrara in 1959. He works as the Policy Officer in charge of multilingualism for the E.U. in Brussels. He writes columns for various European newspapers about current affairs in Europanto, a language that he has invented. His collection of short stories in Europanto, *Las Adventures des Inspector Cabillot* has been published by Dedalus.

Diego has had eight novels published in Italian, including the highly acclaimed trilogy *New Finnish Grammar* (Dedalus 2011), *The Last of the Vostyachs* (Dedalus 2012) and *The Interpreter* (Dedalus 2016) which have found worldwide success. His latest novel, a detective novel with a difference, *God's Dog* was published by Dedalus in 2014.

Judith Landry

Judith Landry was educated at Somerville College, Oxford where she obtained a first class honours degree in French and Italian.

Her translations from Italian for Dedalus are: *The House by the Medlar Tree* by Giovanni Verga, *New Finnish Grammar*, *The Last of the Vostyachs*, *God's Dog*, and *The Interpreter* by Diego Marani and *The Mussolini Canal* by Antonio Pennacchi.

She was awarded the Oxford-Weidenfeld Translation Prize in 2012 for her translation of *New Finnish Grammar*.

'The facts and characters in this novel are purely imaginary. Any similarity to the names of real people, or real events, is therefore simply a matter of chance.'

In times to come, chaos will reign in Hell itself.

Serbian proverb

I

This is the story of my undoing: of how one single man snatched me from those I loved, from my profession, from my private life, and bore me to my ruin, a prey to confusion and mind-befogging illness. Not that this was his callous aim: he couldn't help himself. He simply failed to notice that he was dragging me into that self-same dizzying abyss into which he himself was hurtling. And it is this very fact that makes my torment all the more unbearable. Today I live as a slave to another man's madness. I see its fearful workings before my very eyes, I am a lucid witness to its utter inhumanity, and nothing prevents me from walking away; but I stay. Because by now, for me, any other life would be still greater madness. So each day I wake up, bow my head wearily and carry on, working through a heartless destiny which has chosen me, of all men, for its experiment. Each day I nurture the wild beast to which I am chained, my mind is like a stone, my thoughts like clefts within it; my body a sloughed skin, staked out with wooden pickets and laid out to dry.

That year, the tulips came up diseased. They wilted on the

grass, rotten and black with gnats. I'd planted them one misty November afternoon, with all the morbid enthusiasm of an artificer laying his mines, and throughout the winter I awaited their explosions. They rotted without ever opening, trickles of rust stippling their stems. That should already have struck me as an omen. All the neighbouring gardens looked stricken, as though blighted by some invisible disease. Foul air wafted from the houses like the breath of some troubled sleeper; green-streaked light fell from a leaden sky. That strange dampness hanging over things – poisoning plants, driving birds from their nests – betokened death. I would see the birds of an evening, fluttering in alarm, perched on the highest branches of the lime tree; the next morning I would find broken eggs and little corpses covered in excrement. Everything seemed to be turning to stone; I began to feel that the only thing that was made of flesh and blood in that whole sorry set-up was myself. But slowly I too was becoming petrified, assuming a mineral heaviness.

At least Irene was still with me then. I had her presence to channel the flow of my days, the rhythm of her breathing to hold my nights together. The fine-tuning between us, in our household intimacy, was so perfect that we had no need for speech. We could communicate by means of sound. When I heard the taps in the upstairs bathroom running, I knew that Irene was going to have a bath, and the time on the clock and the day of the week on the calendar told me the rest: whether it was the cinema or the restaurant that she wanted to go to. In winter, the prolonged creaking of the parquet in the living-room of a Sunday morning was a summons: Irene was sitting on the sofa, waiting for me. We would be going out for an aperitif, or to buy flowers. When I came home late from the office, if I heard the sound of drawers being continuously opened and closed, I knew that she was in a bad mood, or irritated with me because I was late. Then I would put on the television and turn up the volume of the signature tune of our favourite programme to lure her down. On weekend afternoons, if she failed to hear me moving around in my study, it was she who would come up to look for me, throwing open the window and saying: 'It's stuffy in here!' She would take me by the hand and lead me into the living-room, then sit down at the piano and begin to play.

I'd lived a quiet, somewhat circumspect life with Irene for many years. We'd met each other too late in life for our by now hardened sense of solitude to melt away in the warmth of mutual affection. We each nursed our independence as though it were an ageing parent whom we treated abruptly, distantly, secretly chiding it for its dogged capacity for survival. Yet, side by side, we kept each other company in the old house where we had gone to live together. We had rented it almost by way of a joke, a challenge: it was too big for us, too expensive to maintain, and there was too much garden. But those large spaces, those light-filled rooms, served to remind us both of the cramped lodgings of our earlier existences. With time, we'd fashioned those walls to our own shapes. The floors bore the imprint of our passing, the wood was worn from contact with our hands. The light switches and window frames responded to our touch; despite the imperfections that had accumulated over the years, they remained docile and obedient when it was we who pressed upon or raised them. We had become commingled with the essence of that house, with the materials of which it was constructed; its stonework, its panelling, its very dust were impregnated with our being, to the point of giving out our very smell. We in return bore it upon our clothes, it came gusting towards us when we opened the door, back from some holiday. I would sometimes come upon it, when I was travelling for my work, lurking in some handkerchief, or in a book, or in a tie left too long in a cupboard. Over time, Irene had filled the rooms with antique furniture; she had great flair, and would frequently unearth rare or striking pieces. She would spend hours in antique shops she'd come across in some out-of-the-way village across the border, and when she had found something that particularly caught her fancy, she was like a dog with a bone: she'd stroke it and sniff at it, examine handles and hinges, test out the locks, listen to the creaking of the joints, open and close drawers and doors, drumming on the wood with her knuckles. But she would make a purchase only after meticulous deliberation. She would subject the puzzled vendor to lengthy questioning, until she had extracted all that he knew about the history of the item in question; then, when it seemed that the deal was about to be done, she would thank him and be off, saying that she also wanted to give the piece in question time to think. Running the risk of finding it gone, she would return to the shop several days later, at a different time: to take the item by surprise, she would say, because only in its lonely abandonment, stripped of all expectations, would the old wood loosen its fibres and reveal its soul. Her relationship with the furniture that she brought home varied from piece to piece: each one had its own character, and Irene knew how to bring it out. She would introduce them to me like silent relatives who were coming to stay. I always found them faintly disquieting; it seemed to me that they did indeed hold something living prisoner within their boards, and often it would occur to me that perhaps I too had become one of them, an old chest-of-drawers forgotten in some junk shop, and that Irene had chosen me in the same way, touching me, sniffing me, running her hands over my old frame and finding it to be that of a seasoned loner. Yet for me, the presence of their austere forms in that house were so many pointers to Irene's own presence, which was as solid, antique and immutable as their carved wood. Irene and I had lived together for so long that by now she felt like one of my own internal organs. Somewhere within me, there she was, pulsating along with the rest; and our everyday life slid past, as untroubled as a landscape viewed from a train, becoming gradually cluttered up with holiday photos, clothes inevitably soon out of fashion, phases that gently coalesced, memories that could be either hers or mine. But all this was doomed inexorably to end. An invisible worm was silently devouring us from within: beneath the lustrous shell of our apparent happiness, of that precious, ever stronger bond we believed time to have forged between us, all that was left was dust.

One evening during that dismal spring, catching me looking sadly out of the window at my blighted tulips, Irene had come up to me and put her arms around my waist. 'Your roses will make up for them!' she whispered in my ear. I smiled at those words of consolation, but instead of joy, what I felt within me was the cold breath of an unknown fear. A touch of lassitude had crept into her voice, a resigned wariness. At that same moment a brief, light shower of rain spattered the gardens, and an unexpected shaft of sunlight turned the thousand drops upon the window panes an orange-yellow. For some time – as the blue night fell upon the rain-soaked city and entered our friendly house, swelling the shadows and blurring our faces – I held her in my arms.

Over those days – now splintered into a thousand fragments – I was beginning my new job as head of the interpreters' department. It was a world I hardly knew, quite different from that of the administrative duties I'd previously carried out. Geographically, the offices of the conference section of the international body for which I was now working were in something of a backwater, housed in a green suburbia of neat modern roads, in a spacious park, so that my little white building at the end of an avenue of maples looked like a clinic, a sanatorium housing the sufferers from some rare but not dangerous disease. And, truth to tell, working among interpreters, I did indeed feel that I was dealing with 'sufferers', beset by some mysterious unease. Their troubles usually took the form of a garrulous euphoria, but also sometimes that of a scabby touchiness, like an internal itch that could never be assuaged. Without knowing any of them personally, I had learned to distinguish them from among the anonymous crowd of functionaries. In the canteen, in the bar, in the local restaurants, in the entrance halls of our various offices, they formed small groups of wildly gesticulating, wild-eyed individuals, endlessly prattling, leaping from one language to another like acrobats, sometimes prone to fitful movements, reminiscent of those made for no apparent reason by a fish or bird. They did not seem to engage in conversations, I didn't feel that they listened to one another. Their talk had an over-enthusiastic quality about it, like that of witch doctors who are using the word to keep themselves in a state of trance. I came to see that they had a horror of silence; they seemed to stiffen in alarm whenever they sensed that it was about to descend upon them. They fended it off with an animal instinct, clustering in noisy packs. Even when meetings went on until late at night, and in the breaks when I would come upon them at the counter in the bar, bleary-eyed and drowsy, there was always one who would carry on gabbling, keeping the fire of the word alive so as to ferry his companions out of that cold and silent hour. The others would listen to him trustingly, abandoning themselves to his voice as though to a life-saving raft.

In my heart of hearts, I've always had trouble with polyglots. Above all, because those who vaunt a knowledge of many languages have always struck me as show-offs. No human being can really be capable of speaking the tongues of so many others equally well; anyone venturing to do so is embarking on an unhealthy exercise which can only lead to mental instability. The only foreign language known to me is an inadequate and obsolete German, acquired willy-nilly at grammar school. My father's mother tongue has never put down roots in me; if I can still drag up some stilted phrases, this is not because I practise it or take care to keep myself updated in this tongue that I find so antipathetic, but simply because – behind the hazy memory of rules learned off by heart, like answers at a catechism class – I can still hear my father reproving me in his own exasperated German. I hear my teacher imperiously summoning me to the blackboard for questioning, browbeating me, ordering me to speak German, as a soldier might be ordered out of a trench to go on the attack. It matters little that the threat has passed; the fear remains; only such fear could induce a man to leave his own mind unguarded to pursue words that are not his. Languages are like toothbrushes: the only one you should put into your mouth is your own. It's a question of hygiene, of good manners; it's dangerous to let yourself be contaminated by the germs of another tongue. What do we know about what might be unleashed when they slip into the delicate vessels of our brain, when they mingle with our most ancient juices and generate some hybrid that God never intended? The germs of European diseases did for the American Indians. Similarly, a foreign language injected into our mind brings with it the taint of unknown sounds, a vision of worlds that are incomprehensible to us – the lure of other truths and a devilish desire to know them.

That was why I was alarmed by the swarm of ranters I was now being called upon to manage. They were people who challenged God; who, out of sheer devilry and vanity, would lean forward to peer into the abyss of madness. They struck me as circus performers, shifty, dishonest quick-change artists, mental stuntmen, who at any moment might put a foot wrong and take a serious fall. In truth, if I had agreed to go and run the interpreters' department, it was simply because I felt I should do my superiors' bidding. None of my colleagues wanted that thankless task, no one wanted anything to do with that horde of touchy, lying prima donnas. But I, with the vague promise of some more prestigious future post, had allowed myself to be persuaded. I hadn't managed to say no. Even Irene said I was a fool. She accused me of going to the office as to a barracks, of performing my job like some blinkered soldier, who carries out the most fatuous corvée without batting an eyelid. She was right. I wore my grey functionary's suit like a uniform, I was proud of my soldierly career as an anonymous executive. In my Spartan office, amidst the metal furniture and two-tone filing cabinets, I felt safe from the capricious world outside. I was fond of my office and its shabby furnishings; what I liked about it was that it had no history, no character, it was not even mine. It could be taken apart and put up again in a thousand other places without ever absorbing anything of the humanity amidst which it stood; the complete opposite of Irene's furniture: laden with suffering, blackened by time and shot through with dead voices which, on certain nights, I felt I could hear emanating from the wood and peopling the house with ghosts, with lost souls, forever held back by time's stealthy undertow. Whereas, in my own office, nothing ever happened which wasn't caused by me. Everything had its routine, everything was governed by iron rules which protected me from the humiliation of doubt. Safe in my glass barracks, I commanded a gigantic army, with rows of string-bound files in place of tanks, and reams of paper doing duty for bombs, capable of destroying men and things in total silence. I did not know that what would be destroyed – by the few fussy, handwritten lines on a piece of lined paper referred to as Report 99/5162 which I found on my desk that windy March morning – would be me.

Note to the Director, Interpreters and Conferences Department

Subject: Mr. XXX: Professional behaviour and performance.

It is reported that, despite continual reprimands and warnings (see previous notes of XXX September and XXX January), Mr. XXX , civil servant, grade L/4, continues to be remiss in the performance of his duties, and harbours attitudes that are unsuited to his rank and function.

In the present case, we are informed that Mr. XXX, while engaged in his work as a simultaneous interpreter, emits completely meaningless sounds and whistles; he translates inattentively, adding words of his own invention, which do not figure in the speaker's speech; he indulges in long pauses, interrupting the translation, and expresses himself in languages other than those required for the meeting in question.

In the present context, attention should be paid to the view put forward by Dr. Herbert Barnung concerning the psychic health of the above, pointed out in an attachment to note n. 16/00, as well as the following notes from the health committee. Bearing in mind his record, and in view of the joint committee's note 3/408 and articles 41, 64 and 82, section 3, subsection of the internal regulations, we invite the appropriate authority to take suitable steps in this connection, namely, for Mr. XXX's immediate suspension from duty.

Gunther Stauber
Head of Department

Gunther Stauber was a ruddy-faced German with thinning straw-coloured hair. Huddled awkwardly on the armchair in front of my desk because of his girth, he kept crossing and uncrossing his legs, his shirt billowing out at every laboured breath. He tried to offset the massiveness of his frame with an attempt at military bearing which, rather than rendering him more authoritative, in fact made him look like a lion-tamer. He looked on impatiently, waiting for me to take my eyes off the hefty bundle of papers the secretary had laid out for me on the table.

'As you well know, ours is an arduous task. For eight hours a day we spin our brains around as though in a blender. We grind the words of one language down into a fine paste so as to refashion them into those of another; and each word that enters our ears sooner or later will have to issue from our mouths. In the evening, as we leave our booths, it takes a bit of time for our brains to slow down to a normal speed; we need to shut down the machine, take everything to pieces, clean the machinery and let it rest, oiling the screws. But with age, and professional wear and tear, sometimes some people just can't turn off the engine; so the brain carries on idling. The pieces get worn out, the spools overheat and the mouth spits out not real words, but everything that has got caught up in the gears – remains, dross, the residue of speech. Ultimately, the blade is blunted; it no longer cuts. It balks at the harder words, beheading them without properly grinding them. They go into the machine and come out mutilated, distorted, but not translated. They are unrecognisable. This is what has happened to our colleague.'

Instinctively, I raised my hands to rub them over my temples; I suddenly had the unpleasant feeling that I too had something electric running around in my cranium.

'But don't you think your colleague just needs a bit of a break?' I objected cautiously. Stauber sniffed disdainfully and stiffened on his seat.

'He's had a bit of a break, as you put it, on more than one occasion. It's all there in the file – three long periods of leave for health purposes. In fact, his psychiatrist insisted on it.'

He sounded irritated, as though these were things he'd already said a hundred times.

'Do you really think his behaviour is unacceptable? After all, he's still a pro. Very well-trained, and highly experienced. Can't we just wait? And, in the meantime, head him off to less important meetings, where he can do less harm? Some debate at a seminar, nothing technical and not many languages involved?' was my next suggestion.

'Less important meetings? Impossible! What with his grade, if we don't send him to ministerial meetings he hits the roof! Prickly as a pear, that's what he is. He'll never admit that he's ill, and he certainly won't agree to being considered a category two interpreter! If I assign him to meetings where there are fewer than five languages involved, he goes ballistic. He starts writing me notes saying that his abilities are going to waste, and has them sent to all the directors-general! More to the point, our department's good name is at stake. When an interpreter starts raving into the microphone, no matter how insignificant the meeting, people get to hear of it. The delegates complain. We receive written protests from ambassadors. We can't afford to wait. Even his colleagues can't take much more!'

Stauber was becoming increasingly indignant. Now he straightened up and wiped his forehead with his handkerchief. I stood up and walked towards the window. A stiff breeze was causing the clouds to fray and leave icy trails behind them in the sky. Splashes of yellowish sunlight suddenly fell over the room; without warming them, they gave things a dusty, transient look. They lit up the photo of Irene in its silver frame on the desk. The trams were glittering in the roads below; slowly, laboriously, the city was coming back to life.

'I imagine you know this colleague well. He too is German; he must be about your age. From the records, I see that you were both taken on in the same year. Tell me a bit about his private life. Slip-ups and all. You must know a thing or two. What was he like as a young man? Even he must have been a bit more easy-going in his youth! He can't always have been so disturbed. I see from his file that he never married; but he might have had girlfriends, and he must have had a family and friends. Apart from languages, he must have had other interests. I don't know, some hobby or other. Sport, perhaps?' My thoughts turned with relief to my tulips and roses; they were surely a fig-leaf against madness. Stauber heard me out, though he was clearly dying to interrupt.

'Sport, hobbies, friends – forget it! He's always been just as he is today. He arrived here twenty years ago with that same wooden look on his face, eyes glazed over with that same anguish, glaring with that same steely determination – to do what, I've no idea. He had something of the spy about him, of the hired assassin. But then at least he didn't make mistakes.

His simultaneous translations were like radio bulletins; his voice was harsh, almost threatening, demanding attention. I remember that some delegates were in awe of him; they'd listen to him through the headphones and then crane their necks to look into the booths, wondering who it was who was speaking in such severe, commanding tones. You're right, he is German, but his family isn't from Germany; I think they're from some Balkan country. He doesn't drive, he doesn't smoke, and all he drinks is water. He spends his holidays travelling the world, doing language courses; he's lived alone in the same furnished flat for twenty years. No one knows much about him; he hasn't any friends – well, certainly not at work. He always has lunch in the canteen, alone, reading the paper, in a different language each day; and I know that he always has supper in a restaurant near his flat, at seven on the dot. It's by my bus stop, and when I come home late I see him sitting at his usual place in front of a glass of water, lost in thought, with some strange paper spread out before him. On a few occasions I've bumped into him in town of an evening, together with a woman, though never the same one. Although…'

He crossed his legs and put two fingers to his collar to loosen his tie.

'Although?' I encouraged him.

'Although not even then did I ever see him smile! I never saw him looking animated, or affectionate or loving. I don't think they were women he went to bed with, I can't see him touching them. He seemed somewhat impatient in their company, as though they were distant relatives passing through town and he had to entertain them for the weekend. Do you see what I mean?'

I nodded. Visibly ill at ease, Stauber was inhaling noisily and wiping his sweaty hands on his trousers.

'Loneliness can play nasty tricks. It can swallow a person up like quicksand,' he added in a calmer voice, then carried on:

'That man has always kept himself to himself. When it came to organising a conference he would say just the bare minimum to his colleagues, then withdraw behind that hypnotic stare of his, as though he'd ceased to see us and we were so many empty chairs. When you talk to him you get the feeling that there's no one actually there, no personality, just a spongy blob of abnormal memory which has achieved its size by swallowing all the other organs of his body, which is now just an empty shell!'

I had summoned the head of the German section in order to sort out this irritating matter as quickly as possible; I was looking for the speediest and, for me, the simplest solution. I felt I was wasting my time on such improbable matters as an interpreter who raves and whistles at random. I had trouble even believing such a tale. But I was beginning to fear that such things would be the stuff of my duties as long as I remained at the head of a department dealing with such madmen. I carried on staring out of the window in order that Stauber should not see the irritation which my expression so clearly betrayed.

'But tell me more about this raving you talk of – what exactly does it consist of?' I asked him, still without turning around.

'We've got recordings of him, if you'd like to hear them! Sometimes he stops translating right in the middle of a speech and starts uttering meaningless words which don't exist in any language, as though he himself were trying to work out how to pronounce them. He turns them over in his mouth to see how they will sound, and scribbles illegible signs down on a piece of paper. Or he'll carry on translating, but in a different language, one that's got nothing to do with that particular meeting. The worst thing is when he starts to make hissing noises, or squawks perhaps, with a kind of whistle coming from the throat. People who've seen him say that at such times he goes completely stiff, craning his neck, lifting his chin and narrowing his eyes, as though he needed to make a special effort at concentration. Luckily, at that point his colleagues usually manage to turn off the microphone without anyone noticing and carry on interpreting themselves. But he carries on chirping, pronouncing meaningless words or blethering sounds in some unknown language. It upsets the meeting, delegates turn round to stare, some even leave the hall, and the speaker stops speaking. And then they blame me! I'm the one who takes the rap. It's me who gets called on to provide explanations!'

His voice rising to a crescendo, he tapped himself on the chest. I turned towards him and asked him brusquely:

'In a word, Stauber, what do you suggest?'

He narrowed his eyes against the sudden burst of sunlight that was now flooding the room. But he remained totally unruffled; I felt that he had had his words prepared right from the moment he entered my office.

'I suggest that he should be suspended forthwith and then, ideally, declared permanently unfit for work. That's within the regulations. All the conditions are in place so no one could object. That way he'd be out from under our feet – and never fear, he'd get a golden handshake, no problem about that. Then he could spend the rest of his life calmly raving away to his heart's content and studying all the languages he likes – there must be one or two he still has to add to his collection – without putting a spanner in our works.'

It was as though a weight had been lifted from him. I went back to my seat. What Stauber wanted from me was a signature.

That would mean that the interpreter could be legitimately suspended from his post, and that the arrangements for dismissal could be set in motion. I was beginning to think that this was the only way out, the only way I could wash my hands of this whole tiresome matter. Yet still I hesitated.

'Wouldn't it still be preferable to see how his illness develops? We have no reason to think that it's permanent; or incurable. He might be able to have some sort of therapy,' I persisted.

Stauber shot me a grim look. He sat bolt upright in his chair and clasped his hands around his knees.

'When the mower breaks down, what do you do? Hope it will mend itself?' he asked sourly before collapsing down again, puffing, into the depth of his chair.

I closed the interpreter's file and placed my clasped hands on the table.

'Let me think about it,' I said, noting that at this point Stauber did not seem to know which leg to put on top of the other. He got up from his chair, straightened his jacket and awkwardly offered me his hand.

'Stauber, how many languages do you speak?' I asked point-blank.

'Five...' he said after a moment's hesitation.

'Which ones?' I persisted.

'Russian, French, English, Italian and Spanish. Why?' he asked gloomily.

'Pure curiosity!' I answered with a smile as I accompanied him to the door. Alone in the room, I sat down again listlessly at my desk. Now the sun was high in the cloudless sky. Lashed by the wind, a distant fuzz of green was softening the sharp horizon, as though the young sap in the new grass and far-off woods were vibrating in the cold air. Shifting Irene's photo slightly so that it would not catch the light, I found myself thinking that all in all, five languages was reasonable enough: Stauber might be a perfectly normal individual.

I had an important meeting in the afternoon. I was to meet the director-general and present my plan for the running and reorganisation of the department. The secretary trotted to and fro, bringing me file after file, each time seeming to expect me to dictate something to her or give her some task to perform; she seemed even less at ease than I was. But I couldn't take my mind off the strange affair of the interpreter. The sound of a telephone ringing in the next-door office brought me down to earth; I drew my seat up to the desk and started to read through one of the files, leafing through the communiques, checking on the internal regulations and the judgements of the joint committee; I even went as far as to read through the hefty psychiatrist's report, and with some care: in the brain of his patient, Dr. Barnung had noted some reduction in the size of the hippocampus and an enlarging of the basal ganglia, together with an abnormal cerebral blood flow. Apparently his age, and certain genetic considerations, put him at risk of schizophrenia. Hallucinations and delirium were the classic symptoms of the illness – he seemed to have the lot: he saw things that weren't there, was afraid that he was being persecuted and convinced that he was gifted with exceptional powers. The psychiatrist even had a specific term for the invention of non-existent words, namely glossolalia – a form of schizophrenia. In this man's one-track life, trouble seemed to have built up like a poison, which had now gradually overflowed from some mysterious vessels to infect his entire brain. Intense mental exercise, study and the general rigour which seemed to have marked his habits had failed to ward off that sly disease, which was now attacking him from within, slowly defeating him like a parasite.

That man knew fifteen languages: French, English, Dutch, Danish, Swedish, Spanish, Portuguese, Greek, Italian, Russian, Polish, Hungarian, Romanian, Japanese and Turkish. German was his mother tongue, but he also interpreted into English. He was forty-seven years old, and had been in the job for twenty-two years. His behaviour and record had been unblemished: no absences, no reprimands. Six months on the waiting list to do a Japanese language course at Tokyo University. He'd been to the best Swiss and German interpreters' schools and had spent long periods of study leave in dozens of countries. Held together by a now somewhat frayed elastic band, he had a collection of university diplomas and testimonials in any number of foreign languages. I paused to look at the photographs: one of a document asking to be entered for some competitive examination, one taken when he first took up his position, later ones of his identity card, renewed every five years. In each one he looked like a different man.

I would come home late in those days, and even spend some time at the office at weekends. In order to reorganise the department I had to make a thorough study of how it worked, to analyse statistics, compare costs and check on the legal underpinnings of the reforms I was preparing to bring in. My promised assistant did not materialise, so I had to do all the work myself. Irene didn't have much patience with this new job of mine; she thought I was being over-zealous. At first, she merely teased me about it.

'You're the only one in that place who's doing two jobs for the price of one! They should give you two pensions; or at least publish two obituaries when you drop dead at your desk of a heart attack!' she would say to me with a bitter laugh when I picked up my bulging briefcase to go to work of a Saturday morning.

But the situation showed no signs of easing up, and I also found myself obliged to take on other duties, attending long and frequent official events at other international institutions in Europe and North America. Irene began to accuse me of deserting her.

One Sunday afternoon, when I had had to go into the office yet again – to trawl through the archives for files relating to some accounts queries – all of a sudden the sky was swept free of clouds, and a burst of sunlight filtered determinedly through the slats of the dusty blinds; and that light told me something, it stirred some memory which warmed my heart. I slapped shut the folders I was looking through, gathered up my things and rushed home. I wanted to take Irene to the lake; we would catch the ferry and go to get a bit of sun on the terrace of an old café where we were regulars. On the way, I broke out into a run, but started sweating and stopped to take off my coat. I dashed into the house, puffing and panting, and called out as I always did, looking up at the white banisters on the stairway. But my voice died away in the emptiness. I went into the living-room, threw my briefcase and overcoat down on the sofa and went up to the first floor. I called out again, thinking that perhaps Irene was hiding, playing a joke on me, as she used to when we were first married. Laughing, I opened the cupboard doors, drew back the curtains around the bed, looked behind doors, certain I'd find her hiding-place. But Irene wasn't there. I went back slowly down the stairs and sat down on the sofa, somewhat concerned by now. In the garden, shaken by a slight breeze, my roses were coming into bud, the dew on them sparkling in the sun. In my mind's eye, I saw the first sails swelling on the lake, the green lawns at its edges teeming with people, the ferry cleaving the foaming water as it approached the jetty where our café awaited us with its peeling paint-work; the only clients at that time of day would be anxious little old ladies wearing white shoes. I looked towards the corridor, straining my ears; I thought I'd heard a noise, but it was just the creaking of old wood. I remember that I dozed off, huddled in my overcoat and, strangely, I remember smiling in my sleep. Irene came into the room, causing the door to squeak, but seeing me asleep she crept away again; I caught a glimpse of her with her raincoat and her umbrella still in her hand. Then all that remained of her was a gust of cold air and the smell of her scent. It was already late; the sun had gone down behind the trees. In the garden, my roses were now still, their heads as stiff and fragile as glass baubles. I could feel the blood beating in my temples and a bluish mist swam before my eyes; I felt cold, numbed by that unnatural sleep. Suddenly I had the irritating feeling of having wasted time; then I felt a cold sadness creeping over me like a snake, slithering over Irene's furniture, slinking under the door and engulfing our whole house in its deathly grip.

A few days later, I found him sitting waiting for me in the brown armchair outside my office. The moment he stood up to greet me I could instantly smell the bitter scent of freshly planed wood which, from then onwards, would always forewarn me of one of his tempestuous visits, or of his hidden presence in various entrance halls, corridors or conference halls; as though he had just passed by, leaving a poisonous odour in his wake. I sat down at my desk and looked closely at that ever labile face which, when I have looked at it for a few moments, even today continues to dissolve before my very eyes, never to be retrieved. It is not a face, it is a mask; tomorrow, today's wrinkles will have changed their course like wadis in a desert; tomorrow, today's pale eyes will have become black empty holes; tomorrow, today's generous mouth will have become a bloodless gash in the cold flesh of a corpse, and tomorrow the silky darkness of his hair will be like stubble, or indeed his skull may now resemble a round bone, monstrously swollen above a neck seamed with black veins.

'What can I do for you?' I would have liked to use his name, but I'd already forgotten it. I hid my embarrassment by fiddling around with the pile of signed and stamped papers from the file which the ever-eager secretary had laid out on my desk.

'It's about the report,' he said, after a fit of coughing.

'Ah, the report…' I pretended not to know what he was talking about and shot him an expectant look.

'Stauber's report – Stauber is my superior,' he explained.

'Tell me more,' I said encouragingly. At first he hesitated, twisting his hands and seeking the first words of a speech he must already have given several times.

'It's nothing but a tissue of brazen lies. It isn't true that I translate badly, or that I utter meaningless words. It isn't true that I'm silent for minutes on end, or that I rave into the microphone – you can come and listen to me if you like. And above all, I'm not ill – so don't dredge up that schizophrenia story again! The psychiatrist can say whatever he likes: I'm the only person inside my head, and only I know what goes on there! As to those sounds, I've explained about them time and again. How can it be that no one will listen to me? They're not senseless noises, they're a language! A secret language! I can hear it swirling through my mind, flowing through my head, cutting across all the rest like a hidden thread! And I repeat those sounds, when they well up, in order to capture that language, to fix it in my mind. I don't know how I became aware of them – probably unconsciously, like so many invisible seeds hidden within the many languages I've studied. Coming together in my brain, they've taken root and sprouted; and now a mysterious language is growing within me without my realising. A process as old as man is taking place in my head: the birth of a new language! Or perhaps the rebirth of an old one, forgotten by mankind!'

His voice had been calm at first, but now it was beginning to sound agitated; the words were pouring from him, angry and forceful. He was seated on the edge of his chair, his forearms on the desk, his hands stretched towards my own as though he wanted to seize them.

'Let's make a pact then, shall we, the two of us?' He made a questioning gesture which demanded a reply. I gave a quick nod. The interpreter took a deep breath and went on:

'Give me time. Just give me time, and I'll find out what's happening, you'll see. Above all, just let me carry on interpreting! It's in the electrolysis of simultaneous interpreting that it all takes place – when words of one language detach themselves like electrons and go swarming off to stick themselves on to another! It's when I hear them vibrating together, all fifteen of them, when their sounds open up like pores, like mucous membranes seeking each other out and recognising each other – it's then, in that fleeting moment of translation, that I hear it surfacing, still faint and distant, it's true, but entire and whole! And when I've tracked it down, when I've understood it more thoroughly and gained a certain mastery of it, then I'll find a way of writing it down. I'll construct its grammar and compile a dictionary; and I'll donate the fruits of my labours to your institute, which will then be able proudly to tell mankind that it is the depository of the language of the universe, the one concealed in the eternal polar ice, the one lurking in the chasms of the oceans, the one which has commanded matter since the dawn of time!'

As he spoke, the veins in his neck were contracting and snapping in his throat like whips. Thinking back to that first encounter, to that first time I witnessed the contortions of that face, all that I remember are two blue veins and the bruised aperture of a mouth.

I lowered my eyes, desperately seeking for something to say. It was clear that the man before me was deranged. I had to find the words to placate him, to distance him from me, and I had to do so as delicately as possible. I pretended to be absorbed in a page in his file while I considered my position. I took a deep breath, bent my head, prepared a smile and raised my face to him, somewhat uncertainly.

'Don't you worry. I'll have a word with Stauber and everything will be sorted out!' I interrupted whatever it was he seemed to want to say by getting up and showing him to the door.

'There's no cause for alarm. Civilised people can always come to an understanding, can they not?' I added for further reassurance, whilst steering him politely but firmly out of the office. He put up no resistance, thinking perhaps that as yet I knew nothing of his case.

'You will tell Stauber that I'm not mad, won't you?' he repeated as he stamped off down the corridor, his footsteps ringing on the lino. I closed the door, exchanging relieved glances with my secretary. I went back to my desk and sat there motionless for quite some time, staring at the empty chair in front of me and listening to the rain pattering against the window panes.

That afternoon I had a bit of free time, so I had myself driven to the conference centre, a luxurious modern building with large windows overlooking the lake, all pink-veined marble and expensive carpeting. I went up to the piano nobile and into a conference hall. The languages being translated were listed on a board; I glanced from the balcony at the seats in the amphitheatre, where the delegates were seated behind the plaques with the names of their countries, their hands on their earphones. A metallic chatter, muffled by the large windows, vibrated senselessly through the air, dying away into the wood panelling on the walls. The door leading to the interpreters' booths was open. I went up four lavishly carpeted steps and turned into the narrow corridor which ran around the hall, with the interpreters' booths opening off it. In each one I saw the shadows of two interpreters, one bent over the microphone, the other listening attentively. And now those glass niches, set into the wall, suddenly struck me as resembling the cells in a laboratory used for storing the valves of primitive organisms, each consisting of just one mouth and one ear, sheathed by vague liquid filaments. I found an open door and an empty booth next to the one used by the French interpreters, slipped into it and peered through the blue-tinted glass. Below me, an usher was walking among the seats, distributing leaflets. The delegates were leafing through their papers and exchanging nods; from time to time one would raise his hand to ask to speak. I took the headphones off the hook, held them up to one ear and turned the knob to hear the various speakers. Voices and languages alternated like so many radio stations from distant countries. The speaker was reading out his piece with his eyes on his audience, and the interpreters would follow him through their microphones. Intrigued, I sat down on the chair and put both earphones on; I tried the French channel first, leaning forwards to observe the interpreter in the next booth whose voice I was hearing: he too was leaning forwards slightly as he spoke, clenching and unclenching his fists as he did so, but his facial expressions did not follow the intonation of his speech, as if the voice that was speaking did not inhabit that body but was simply passing through it, using its vocal cords, its lips, its palate in order to become sound. I looked at his eyes and saw in them a kind of blindness, a fixed, blank, inhuman look, as though he were seeing the unspeakable and could not look away. That cold world I had just glimpsed filled me with fear. I pushed back my chair, turned the knob and listened for a moment to the German. Then I happened upon some unknown language, the merest burble of sound that echoed in my ears, sing-song and sugary, possibly oriental. The next one I came upon was harsher, syncopated and unyielding. I turned the knob again, and heard a female voice pronouncing gummy vowels, which seemed to get stuck on her palate, those of a flabby, boneless language, as though set in transparent gristle. My mind on the interpreter's weird ideas, I was foolishly trying to understand languages I had no knowledge of, breaking down words and syllables, intrigued by the thought that it might be possible to find some feature shared by that swarm of jumbled voices. Could there really be any link between them? I fantasised that I might be the person to track it down. I, who knew nothing of languages and hated anything I couldn't understand. Abandoning myself to such fantasies, lulled by the warm female voice I had in my ear, my thoughts wandered back to the pictures of primitive men in my old school books, Egyptian hieroglyphs under a drawing of the pyramids. A vivid image of my German teacher, set between screeching monkeys and brightly-coloured parrots, his lapels spattered with chalk from the declension-strewn blackboard, now swam into my mind; he was pointing his finger at me, pronouncing my name with his annoying accent. I hung the earphones back on the hook and left the booth with a distinct sense of unease. I shook my head, slightly ashamed at having entertained those absurd thoughts even for a moment, at believing that there might be a grain of truth in the interpreter's abstruse theories. No, that man was sick, and had to go – for his own good and for the good name of our institution.

The days that followed were radiant with sunshine; the sky was filled with light until late evening. I would go home on foot, enjoying the warm air, still ringing with birdsong; I would listen to the wind rustling in the new leaves of the trees in the park, the hooting of a distant ferry on the lake. As I walked, through open windows I could see laid supper tables, lit rooms and televisions. In front of my own house I would pause for a moment before going in; pushing open the door, I would invariably dream of finding everything as it once was: the light on in the kitchen, a bunch of fresh flowers in a vase in the hall of a Tuesday, the smell of floor polish of a Friday, the tapping of Irene's heels as she came to meet me, a favourite record playing in the living-room. Each time in fact, I found a different sort of change, and I had to decipher ever unknown signs to work out the circumstances in which I would find my companion: she would emerge from a shadowy sofa or a room where she had been waiting for me, gazing from a window, lost in thought; she would join me in the kitchen, often barefoot; she would rest her elbows wearily on the table and watch me eating, peering out at me from under her fringe.

Sometimes I would catch her still asleep, completely dressed, one leg hanging over the edge of the bed, her handbag still on her arm. On weekends she got up late and would eat no more than a bite of the croissant I had bought her from her favourite bakery at the end of the road; she would leaf through the papers for the entertainment pages, underlining the times that films would be showing at strange cinemas, which was her way of letting me know where she would be going that afternoon. Sometimes I had tried accompanying her, picking up my coat and following her; in the car she would talk of trivia, of how the maid had dyed the sheets pink, about how a curtain in the living-room had come unstitched and what a bore it was going to be to have it mended. But all of our conversations had the inconsequential quality of those you have on the platform just before one of you gets on to a train. On coming out of the cinema, in the blue light of the afternoon streets, my heart would be weighed down with a sadness heavy as lead. And so, with time, I ended up staying at home alone. I would spend my time in the garden, obsessively tending my roses, as though that were the only way that I could hope to salvage my bond with Irene. At the first sign of an insect on the swelling buds I would rush to spray on insecticide, to spread manure and other nutrients; I would cut off any twig that was out of place, fix climbers to their supports, dig up the slightest weed, pull off dead leaves and pointlessly remove the faded petals. Irene was receding further from me every day, and I could do nothing but be witness to such estrangement. I measured it from time to time, registering the length of her silences, the frequency of her absences, the harshness of her ways; secretly, I hoodwinked myself into believing that the careful registering and measuring of this unknown hurt would ultimately reveal its nature and provide me with some antidote.

There was a mist hanging over the lake on the day she went away for good; it rose slowly from the water like a poisonous breath, and spread over the city, still bathed in the warm twilight. I had just returned from a week of travelling for work, I was dead tired and I knew I had the airport's smell of sweat and crowds upon me; but I had no desire to go home. Going up the stairs, I found the living-room empty; Irene's furniture had disappeared; all that remained of the sideboard, the empire-style divan, the Louis Philippe table, were darker patches on the parquet. My own things were scattered all around the room on the floor in the places where the furniture containing them had stood; they now struck me as a brutal resumé of my life with Irene, a scant anthology of what remained of so many years together: a guide book, a crystal vase that had been a birthday present, the television, the hatstand, the transistor radio, a few art books, silver frames emptied of their photographs, an old pack of cards, an ashtray and my collection of jazz records. Irene was in the living-room, standing in front of the window, smoking a cigarette, with her coat on. Even my footsteps sounded desolate as I entered the empty room. In the half-light, I couldn't make out her expression. I put on the lights.

'I've put your scientific encyclopedia in your study,' was all she said, shielding her eyes from the light; and then she very slowly walked away.

Out of sheer weariness, or perhaps I mean cowardice, I ended up by signing the request for the interpreter's dismissal; I felt that my superiors wanted the whole thing out of the way. One May morning I found the same old yellowing file on my desk again; passed from department to department, it had been growing fatter by the week, filling up with all manner of additional documentation and passed from pillar to post. The moment came when all was safely gathered in; now it was up to me to press the button which would clinch matters once and for all; all I had to do was sign my name beneath so many others on the last dog-eared page. I took the top off my fountain pen and gazed pointlessly at the nib; it had been given to me by Irene when I'd been made head of department, and it was when I signed my name in watery blue ink that I thought I had snapped the link between our destinies, his and my own, catapulted two lives out of their orbits, into the dark and empty cosmos which is the dwelling-place of things that never happened, of those mistaken paths which God, seeking to escape from his own abominable creation, bethought himself to take and then foreswore.

From that day onwards, I had no peace. That man was pursuing me: he went out of his way to bump into me, to catch my attention, even for a moment, and harangue me with his pleas; he would plonk himself down in my secretary's office and refuse to budge until I'd heard him out, but then of course I'd have to tell him the same old things: that my decision was forced upon me, that everything militated against him. The psychiatrist's report, and his own behaviour in his post, as recorded by Stauber, left no way out. I encouraged him to resign himself, pointed out that he would be well provided for and that now at last he had all the time in the world for his research. But he wouldn't listen to reason and repeated his entreaty as he always did.

'Quash the decision! You're the only one in a position to do so! It's no skin off your nose!'

After a while, I stopped paying him any attention. When the secretary announced his arrival, I'd leave the office by the other door, but he wouldn't give up. He carried on hounding me, and wherever I was in the building, I knew that sooner or later I'd see him looming in front of me. It had become an obsession. He'd wait for me as I came out of meetings, follow me down corridors and start calling out my name, elbowing people out of his way to catch up with me. I'd even given up my quiet lunches in the canteen in order to avoid him; I'd get on a tram and go and eat in a bistro frequented by boatmen. He'd send me illegible letters which I usually threw straight into the bin, he'd slip messages under my door. I would even find him waiting for me early in the morning at the closed door of my office or outside the lifts. He would pursue me like a beggar, he'd clutch me by the arm, reiterating his wearisome complaints.

'You've given me a death sentence! This way I'll really go mad! Don't you see that they're fooling you? That it's nothing but lies?'

Sometimes he would even pretend to be someone else in order to make contact with me; he would telephone my secretary and disguise his voice, hoping not to be recognised. On some mornings I'd find a date pencilled into my diary, some appointment with a representative of the international association of conference interpreters, or with a journalist from some well-known newspaper, and who would I find in front of me but that man, pig-headed and recalcitrant as ever, disguised by a false name. On each occasion, something imperceptibly different about him – a wrinkle, the set of his mouth – prevented me from recognising him straight away; confused and embarrassed, I would hesitate; consumed by doubt, I would stare at the figure approaching my desk, taking stock of its clothes, its shoes, its bearing, trying to discern some sign that would give a clue as to its identity. Was this really the person who figured in my diary? Or was it the interpreter in one of his many disguises? Fearing to offend some innocent in his place, I would lose precious time. Only when we were practically nose to nose would I recognise him: it was that smell that gave him away, that sudden waft of glue and bitter sap. But it was too late now: there he was, sitting in front of me, fiddling with the papers on my desk as though to thrust his way in among the thoughts that were currently on my mind. And there we'd go again, with him imploring me to reinstate him.

'I need to do simultaneous translation! I need to hear all the languages together! This is the only place where I can do that. Do you see what I'm saying? You're a good man – let me at least sit in during a conference, I promise not to talk, with the microphone off no one will notice me. Just let me search for the secret language – this is the only place it can be heard! These words are not the rantings of a madman! Just give me a month or two, another two hundred hours of simultaneous translation with five booths, and I'll give you proof I'm not talking nonsense. That's where it is – the language mankind has forgotten! Just forget rules and regulations for a moment. Use your head, for God's sake – you're still capable of it. Remember that a functionary in an international institution is working for the good of all mankind, and not for some bureaucracy!'

I was beginning to get worried: that man might become dangerous. I even thought of going to the police. Nor could I understand why, of all the people who had signed the request for his dismissal, I was the only one he was so doggedly pursuing: perhaps because I had been the last to sign? Or because I was the only one who would agree to see him?

One evening I came across him in the road, at the gate to the park I walked through on my way home. It was raining heavily; the lights of the cars turning off along the lake were catching the tops of the trees, which were tossing in the wind. I was hesitating as to whether to carry on by foot, and was about to go down the avenue to the tram-stop when I heard hurried footsteps between the hedges of the gravel path. Thinking it might be some ne'er-do-well, I went towards the gate and turned round defensively, my umbrella at the ready in the dark. And there he was again, pale, shaking, hollow-eyed, mouth agape. He gestured to me, then set off in the direction of the lake. Some obscure force caused me to follow him, and I walked along beside him in the darkness, punctuated occasionally by a flash of yellow headlight. I peered at him out of the corner of my eye, trying to remember what I could of that ever-changing face. Then, looking around the park with its bluish shadows, I felt a sudden pang of fear. That man was mad, he might attack me, even kill me; yet I walked on by his side. There was some unresolved business between us which I simply had to conclude once and for all, and I felt that now was the time. When we came to the lake he stopped and turned towards me. I took a few steps back from the black water – the rain was still hammering down – and took up a position a few steps away from him. He stayed where he was for a few moments, head bowed, then took his hands out of his pockets and lifted his chin. He made an elaborate and completely senseless movement in the air, and it occurred to me that even his gestures were fatuous, deformed by the power of a will which had gone awry. He spoke in the hoarse, rasping voice of a man who has been shouting for too long.

'Not many people understand what I am searching for. Mankind is troubled by the very idea that the earth might have a secret language, and that this language lies hidden within each of our ruptured words; unsettled by the thought that it lives in objects, in animals, within these trees, even in stones, and that the planets speak to each other using it. Mankind refuses to believe it can understand the ancient language of Eden, the one in which the serpent spoke to Adam!'

A gust of wind carried his voice away amidst the rustling of the leaves and the pounding rain. I could no longer hear his words, so I took a few cautious steps towards him as he stood on the gravel of the bank, legs apart, shouting and gesticulating wildly. It was then that I realised that he was no longer talking in French, or not in French alone. Other sounds with which I was unfamiliar were creeping into his speech. I moved a little nearer: now I could understand again, or at least grasp some phrases.

'You won't be seeing me again, I promise you. I'll keep out of your way – for ever. But I'd like you to know that your imperviousness to my pleading means that you carry a burden of guilt. By being so obtuse, you are doing violence to your own intelligence. You are refusing to understand: you could see through this darkness, and you choose to remain blind. Yet you're complicit in my discovery whether you like it or not, and what you refuse to know will dog you always! All your life you will continue to wonder what I was looking for, and whether I found it. Like me, you know the secret mankind is not yet ready to receive and, like me, you will not be spared. This is the poisonous knowledge I bequeath you! So here they are, the sounds that will torment you from this day forward! Listen! You will hear them in your sleep, they will taint your words, they will pursue you in your loneliness each time the hollow human voices around you become stilled, because these sounds...'

His speech was borne off on another gust of wind. But when the branches stopped creaking and the leaves fell silent in a temporary lull, it was then, with my own eyes and my own ears – I swear to God – that I witnessed the ghastly scene of that man's metamorphosis, one in which all the awful power of creation was at work. His eyes were raised towards the dismal sky, his mouth agape; drawing his stomach in, he began to hiss, emitting a sound like a liquid whistle, which his palate was trying to restrain but which then sank down into his throat and mingled with a raucous vibration of his vocal cords. Between a series of fitful spasms which caused him to seize up, as though in a fit of retching, the mysterious sound gurgled out from behind his glottis to become a muffled whimper, then rose again like overflowing liquid, then exploded into the hollow of his mouth in meaningless, truncated words, apparently uttered by someone else. A prey to uncontrollable grimaces, he nonetheless seemed to embrace the trauma with which he was bedevilled, as though almost welcoming those violent gulps and hiccups into his racked frame. He was grinding his teeth, his eyes were almost out of their sockets, his lips were stretched into a fearful sneer which at times resembled a smile. Animal cries, strident braying, harsh-sounding meaningless words which could belong to no human tongue poured forth, apparently at random. His face too had become transformed, taking on the appearance of a bird, his nose now resembling a beak, his eyes like sightless bubbles of glass; he was waving his arms around in the air like the talons of a bird of prey, and by so doing he seemed to have stirred up the very elements, which now started to whirl around again as though in sympathy. Behind his back, the water was heaving and roiling, as though the sounds he was uttering were striking deep into its dark depths, awakening chill lake monsters from their age-old sleep as they heard his voice from where they lurked in the slime, and rose clumsily to the surface to see who on earth could be calling them.

Aghast at the sight of that fearful vision, I took a step backwards, stumbled through the trees, emerged on to the muddy grass and carried on running until I reached the lighted road.

II

The summer went by like a fit of fever; the offices emptied
out, the corridors now peopled only by the odd dead-eyed
caretaker. The endless papers which, until a few days ago, had
been whirling around on my desk, suddenly calmed down and
became silent. The lake was alive with sailing-boats, leaving
foaming ripples in their wake. A persistent festive buzz came
from its glittering shore, though without ever reaching the city,
which lay silent and crushed beneath the sun's resolute glare. I
sought shelter from all this intrusive brightness by burrowing
into my solitude, surprised to discover how deep I could dig;
I came upon caves of fear and silence where time oozed forth
in slow and heavy drops. I cowered there, anxious to emerge
yet drawn to their chill depths. By day I wandered through the
half-empty city with the excuse of making pointless purchases;
I would buy bread which would then harden, forgotten on my
desk, fruit which would moulder and rot in the plastic bag.
Although I didn't admit as much, it was Irene whom I was
hoping to meet. I would follow every woman who looked
remotely like her, catch up with her, already knowing that

she was not the person I wanted her to be, walk past her and wander off disconsolate, talking to myself like a mad man.

It was the park that I preferred for my solitary ramblings; I would walk, head bowed, along the lakeside, until the call of a seagull or a hooting ferry roused me from my aimless drifting. I'd sit down wearily on a bench, pondering the route of my bleak return. Each hour of the day, each district, recalled a thousand memories, which flew off like flocks of birds at my approach, leaving foul feathers scattered on the grass, all that remained of what had once been such rich swag. Everything fled from me, but everything also pursued me, doggedly. In the deepest shade of the park I sometimes thought I heard the interpreter's squawking and braying and, to my alarm, would find that I had ended up at that very place on the lake shore where I had seen him last. I would hurry off, trying to resist the temptation to turn round, and when at last I yielded, all that I saw was the sun's fitful dazzle on the flower-filled shore and the brightly-coloured ice cream van slithering along the gravelled alleyway with its mournful peal of bells. A breath of fear would ripple through the wet grass, the feeling that something fateful had happened just at that very moment and that I was the only man in the world who was unaware of it. I would be seized by the certainty that something awesome had occurred, but I did not know what; all I felt was the need to remember, to note the light, the colour of the sky, the time, the landscape. So that at least would remain for me.

At night I would lock myself up in the big empty house. The only room I now used was my study; I'd put a camp-bed in it, and would lie there for hours, staring up at the sky until the light drained away and darkness reigned at last. I would doze off, briefly, only to be hounded by the start of a nightmare in which Irene's reproaches would mingle with obscure threats from the interpreter, dragging me from the lukewarm waters of sleep. Since the interpreter had no clearly-defined face, it was she who would begin to bark at me, cawing, hissing, staring at me with the eyes of a wild beast, uttering senseless words, like those of a sorceress. I would lie there for hours, drowsing uneasily like a creature beached on scorching sand, racked by fits of exhausted, dry-eyed weeping; only at dawn did I manage to fall asleep for a few hours, to wake up cold and aching, my head still full of the gibberish that had peopled my nightmares, which I repeated to myself mechanically – against my will, it seemed to have become lodged in my tangled memory, to have cemented itself into my mind. On my walks through the park, I would find myself uttering these senseless words out loud, in time to the rhythm of my steps, of my breath, of the music of popular songs played on the radio; they bored themselves insistently into my brain, prolonging night-time anguish into the daylight hours. I even tried putting them side by side, to see if, aligned with one another, they would take on any sense. I broke them down, turned them around, read them backwards, covered whole sheets of paper with them. I went to look them up in foreign dictionaries I'd found in the translation department library.

Sometimes, on my way home, it seemed to me that Irene had been back, that she'd come to look for me while I was out. I went through every room in the house, following imaginary traces of her passing, but all that I found was the dull whiteness of dust on the parquet, the stale scent of my lost peace of mind lingering in some corner. In her pursuit, I combed the city from side to side; I called all the numbers in the little notebook she'd left beside the phone, only to be answered by hairdressers closed for the holidays, cabinet-makers, junk shops, the tinny tones of answerphones in empty flats. I even phoned some relatives of hers in Zurich; her cousin told me she'd gone back to Canada, but no, he didn't have her address; his hesitant tone made me suspect that he was seeking advice from someone else in the room, and I had the sudden feeling that Irene was there, right next to him, prompting him as to what to say. I was assured that he would give her my message, that he would let me know her address in Canada, but while I was dictating my own address into the receiver I had the distinct feeling that it was not being taken down; her cousin seemed very eager to hang up, saying goodbye evasively and with false courtesy. I called the number again many times over the following days, at various times of the day and night; it was answered just once, after many rings, late that same August, by an irritated-sounding maid, who told me in German that there was no one home, they'd all gone to the seaside.

Whole days would go by without my saying a word to a soul; I was surprised to learn how long one could live without speaking. I'd say 'Good morning' to the caretaker in the office, the odd 'sorry' to someone on the tram, a 'thank you' in the bar, and it would already be evening. The trees were turning with the first heavy rain, the nights were becoming dark again; less dramatic dawns would reveal a steely sky which sent a fine white dust raining down on to the city, and the lake was puckered with cold wrinkles, which broke up on the shore like the laboured breath of a sick man. Voices rang out again in office corridors and the streets were bright with headlamps of an evening. I started work again, and within the shelter of my room the grip of solitude eased up a little; in there, time could flow over me without harming me. But as soon as I was out again on the street, I felt myself short of breath, each corner like a dagger of anguish planted in my back. I'd try to spin out my journey, to put off the moment when I'd have to turn the key in the lock and be enveloped by the darkness of those empty rooms. I'd wander from one pavement to another, sometimes suddenly changing direction to escape my goal, and I had the feeling that the people around me noticed my odd behaviour and looked at me suspiciously, as though I were a beggar.

It happened for the first time on a Saturday afternoon, and in the moments that followed I truly felt that each man and his destiny are two sworn enemies whom only death will part; only one of the two can go on living, the other must succumb. The fight is not only desperate, it is also unequal; it may go on for years, or draw to a lightning close. Yet there are men who manage to floor their mortal double and clear the way for their own existence. I am not one of them: I died that day, and the person who is writing this is a mere ghost. I'd gone into a baker's to buy my usual loaf of bread, but instead of the words I had intended to produce, what came out of my mouth was incomprehensible blather. At first I thought I was just out of practice, that my long periods of silence had weakened my powers of conversation; in the office I'd already noticed my voice becoming hoarse after just a few moments dictating to my secretary. So I simply gave the puzzled shop-girl an embarrassed look and tried repeating my request. In my efforts to speak clearly, I felt my throat knotting up; between the words I was so clumsily pronouncing, I gave out a long rasping sound like that of a whimpering dog. Eyes wide with terror, I backed off towards the door and left the shop, making brusque gestures of refusal to the alarm-stricken shop-girl who was still firmly proffering me my loaf of bread. I ran off like a murderer, my throat paralysed by fear, turning around every so often to look back at the by now distant baker's to check that no one was coming after me, that people were not stopping to point at me as I passed. When I got home, I rushed up panting to the bathroom mirror: what I saw reflected before me was not my usual gaunt face, but one with the glassy eyes of a fish, a foam-flecked mouth like the jaws of a wild beast, and the rough and scaly skin of a reptile – a constant succession of metamorphosing animals, not one of them containing anything of my original self. I drew what breath I could and bared my teeth to pronounce my name: 'Felix Bellamy! I'm Felix Bellamy, born in Geneva on June 13th 1950!' I shrieked at the top of my voice, and only then did I burst into tears. Terrible days followed: I no longer dared to speak. In the office I pretended to have lost my voice, I addressed my secretary in monosyllables, or using words I'd cautiously tried out beforehand, outside the door. At home in the evenings I'd read out loud from some work document, to see how serious the problem was – I could feel it spreading ominously within me. Inevitably it would recur: just when I felt the warm flow of words running evenly and freely from my throat, suddenly they would crumble into contorted syllables, become guttural stuttering sounds, then whistles. I tried to resist this transformation with all my might, twisting my neck, raising my chin, grinding my teeth, thrusting my tongue vainly backwards to free it from the knot which was throttling it at its root. But in the end all that remained of my voice was a raucous shout, gurgling like vomit from some unknown breach in my glottis. It all happened almost without my noticing, as though some other being had taken temporary possession of my mouth to use it as its own – some unknown and monstrous being which had made its way into my body and was struggling laboriously to come out into the world.

It didn't take me long to realise what had happened. I was ill, I could no longer hide the fact. The illness that had found its home within me was a parasite, a sort of fungus, an unthinking worm, made up of merciless cells which would devour me if I did not have some recourse to action. But was it not already too late? After much hesitation, remembering the psychiatric report attached to his medical notes, I decided to go to the archives and look for the file on the interpreter. I wanted to track down the specialist who had diagnosed his illness and put myself in his hands – before it was too late, for me as well. On the last page of the file I found the name and address of Dr. Herbert Barnung, a German expert who had done years of research into language disorders.

I left for Munich one muggy day in late summer. The airport was extremely quiet; the girls at the cash-desks in the duty-free shops were twirling around on their stools, underemployed, shoes off, scratching one heel with the big toe of the other foot, and inspecting their nails. In the corridors leading to the flight decks, the only sound was the customs-men's radios crackling behind the plate-glass of their cabins. Once I'd boarded the plane, the mood seemed to be one of intense expectation: peering at the faces of the other passengers, absorbed in their newspapers, I had the impression that we were all going to see Dr. Barnung. His consulting room turned out to be in the new part of the city, at the edge of extensive woods and lawns dotted with flowerbeds. What I particularly remember of that warm and sunny afternoon is the outline of a cat crouching on the sill behind the tinted glass of a window giving on to the garden, the long shadows cast on the wall by the seats in the waiting-room, the old magazines on the table and Dr.

The Interpreter

Barnung himself, thin and pale in his white gown, coming towards me and holding out his hand, yet at the same time somewhat forbidding, with the spare look of a military man used to a frugal life-style. He had hard features, prominent cheekbones, a high, freckled forehead; behind his clear blue eyes I sensed the shadow of distant trouble, the force of an iron will. His consulting room had heavy wooden panelling and dark, heavy furnishings; on the walls, in ornamental metal frames, were large prints of birds of prey. Clasping his long white hands together and rubbing them along the table, he listened attentively to my tale of woe. When I embarked on the unlikely story of the interpreter and his secret language, contrary to my expectations, he neither interrupted me nor seemed to become impatient. He read carefully through the pages on which I had written out the meaningless words that punctuated my nightmares, pausing for thought, knitting his thick reddish eyebrows; at times he would glance up from his reading and scan my face with an impassive look. I was not to have long to describe my problems, however, because I soon found myself beginning to stammer out my gibberish in front of him as well; my tongue became glued to my palate, and when at last I managed to loosen it from the grip of the cramp that had mysteriously assailed it, I found my throat seizing up, driving out the air I was vainly drawing in from my lungs in my efforts to articulate my words, yet turning them into nothing more than warbling babble. Alarmed, Dr. Barnung put a finger to his lips, then appeared to smile, perhaps the smug smile of a professional who has identified the problem. He wrote some notes in minuscule handwriting, glancing up occasionally in fascination to observe the spasmodic contractions of my face as he did so. But when at last he spoke, his expression was impenetrable and his voice grave.

'Do you have difficulty in focussing on what you're looking at? Do you sometimes suddenly find yourself right up against things which seconds before had seemed far away?'

'I don't know. But my vision does cloud over, and I do have long periods of distraction which I can't then reconstruct.'

'What is your mother tongue?'

'French.'

'Are other languages spoken in your family?'

'My paternal grandparents were German; but I never knew them.'

'Did your father speak German with you?'

'Not often. He never taught me. He used German mainly when it was something serious, or to tell me off. I understood it, but I couldn't speak it.'

'Did you answer your father back when he scolded you in German?'

'No. I never answered back. Indeed, it was to let me know that I mustn't answer back that he spoke to me in German.'

'Did your mother speak any language apart from French?'

'She too could understand German, but she didn't speak it.'

'Not even with your father?'

'No.'

Dr. Barnung nodded, pursed his lips and pushed away the paper with his tiny writing. Clasping his hands again, he put his elbows on the table.

'Mr. Bellamy, in all probability, what you are suffering from is a serious linguistic dissociation. We'll need to have other sessions to sort the matter completely, possibly using hypnosis, but it seems clear to me that a split between French and German has opened up in your unconscious; between the language you habitually spoke, and the one associated with serious occasions, and not answering back. This dichotomy has caused a disturbance which you have hitherto managed to keep under control; but, for some unknown reason, something has occurred which has upset your delicate psychic balance. Your mind can no longer tolerate this disconnect and is expressing its suffering by emitting incoherent sounds; it must have sensed that the root of the problem lies in your relationship with your parents. At one time such psychoses could only be tackled with the brutal chemistry of psychiatry, or with the slow and complex processes of psychoanalysis. In our clinic, we have developed forms of therapy which are less disruptive and more decisive, thanks to which you will not have to delve into your unconscious in search of painful buried memories. All that you will need to do to cure your disease is to monitor the tracks which French and German have traced in your mind, widening them where they have become constricted and stemming them in the places where they overflow. With the help of the sophisticated technique of linguistic hypnosis we use in this institute, you have excellent chances of recovery. Sometimes just a few weeks' therapy is enough to relieve the symptoms, but for a lasting recovery more time is needed. You will have to be with us for some time, and submit yourself to our cure willingly and constructively if you truly want to get better.'

I glanced up at the doctor incredulously. For a moment I thought that I had fallen victim to an elaborate hoax. Perhaps our conversation had been a sort of dress rehearsal to which he had to subject unknown patients who turned up in his clinic in order to distinguish mythomaniacs from those who were really ill. I smiled awkwardly, to show him that I had seen through his ruse and that we could now proceed to the real interview. But that chill stare, the marble coldness of that angular body, which seemed to spread to every object in the room, made me realise that Dr. Barnung was not joking; that he had never joked in his whole life, that for him every form of existence was a kind of madness to be cured. I would have liked to laugh in his face, to have accused him of being a charlatan and run out into the sunlight, away from that airless room. But deep down I felt that the doctor was right, that there was indeed something hanging open and unstitched within me; weakened by that invisible haemorrhage, my mind was becoming dimmer, spinning out of my control, slowly dissolving, making me easy prey to the other beings who now lived within me.

'And what do your cures consist of?' I asked meekly, a large knot forming in my chest.

'Of language courses, Mr. Bellamy. You see, for us each language has its own therapeutic value; we make the most of all its virtues. For curing the most extreme pathologies, we do not flinch from recourse to using the rarest and most difficult of all. Of course, the point of departure is always the patient's mother tongue. Something that might be of benefit to a Chinese person might do you irrevocable psychic harm but have no effect at all upon a speaker of Bantu. So here in this clinic the patients are rigorously subdivided into separate linguistic departments. There can be nothing more harmful, at this stage in the cure, than exposing a patient to a language to which he is unsuited.'

'And what is the language for me?'

'The right language is determined by the pathology, but it may change as the cure proceeds, depending on the degree and speed of the recovery. In your case, what I'd suggest first is an intensive course of Romanian. You see, French and German are similar in the way they view reality, but in essence they are profoundly different. Latin and Germanic languages have something in common, they may influence one another and, with time, even understand each other; but they cannot mix. Romanian on the other hand is a happy synthesis between Slav and Latin; in Romanian, all that is rational about Rome, mingled with Mediterranean ebullience, becomes fused with irrational Slav passion and melts into the yearning melancholy of the steppe. Association with this balanced medley of language and spirit will do you good, it will help to heal the wound you currently feel throbbing in your mind. The healing process will take place unconsciously. By sinking deep into the meanders of your brain, the learning of this new language will make good the damage. Alongside the Romanian cure, however, I'd also suggest protracted German therapy, partly because for us German is a bit like aspirin, it's good for everything: it clarifies thought processes, stiffens resolve and lays feelings bare. In your case, it is also one of the branches of your mind which you must rediscover and learn to live with: there is an atrophied residue of German within you which is clinging on to life, but which might also end up by obstructing your psychic development. I feel I must warn you that complications could arise. Disturbed by a sudden feeling of estrangement, at first your ego might take refuge in French and refuse to emerge from it, and then shock therapy would be required. We would have to subject you to a deeply alienating and, how can I put it, exotic linguistic soaking, with some sessions of Tungusic and Inuit to lure your ego out and oblige it to face up to the trauma it is suffering. Occasionally we might even have to have recourse to dead languages: the primitive structure of languages such as Matagalpa and Tuscarora can sometimes jolt the worn mechanisms of modern languages back into action, affording the mind the possibility of a fresh start. Therapeutically speaking, such steps are the equivalent of electric shock treatment. Don't worry, though, we resort to such methods only in extreme cases.'

In the glancing light, Dr. Barnung's face was a red eyeless mask; he was moving his mouth in an unnatural fashion and to me his voice sounded distorted, like the sound of a radio whose batteries are running down. There was a pause; he moved away from the window and into the bluish half-light.

'What would happen if I didn't undertake a cure? I mean, what risks do I run if I leave it to my mind to find its way on its own?'

I was having trouble breathing, seized as I was with a sense of powerlessness which almost prevented me from inwardly expressing any astonishment at the doctor's bizarre theories.

'Linguistic confusion; followed shortly afterwards by mental confusion. That is what awaits you if you take no action. You have come to me today with a wound too deep to heal by itself; if you ignore it, it will become infected and contaminate the healthy tissues too. Mental wounds do not produce blood or scabs or pus; the pain they cause is invisible and unbearable. Faced with such suffering, your brain will lock itself away in the only place of refuge left to it: in madness.'

Spoken at the fateful hour of sunset, those words frightened me but at the same time reassured me. I knew at last that I was indeed ill. In my heart I felt my resolve stiffening; I would follow the doctor's advice to the letter. My cure would be a sort of purge: I would be cleansed of all the evil that had been building up within me and I would also be cured of the poisonous memory of Irene.

Dr. Barnung was looking at me in silence; I could hardly make out his expression, the room had grown so dim.

'I realise that you must find what I have told you deeply puzzling. I suggest that you take time to think things over, go home and let a few days pass. In the meantime, I'll be happy to give you any clarifications you may feel you need. Don't hesitate to phone me if you want to. It is vital that patients have complete faith in the therapy we offer them, and also that they do exactly what we tell them when they have agreed to go ahead. It is crucial that it should be you who makes the decision, that you do indeed truly want to be cured and that you are completely happy to have put yourself into our hands.'

The first thing that came into my mind, as I listened to him, was that the interpreter too must be suffering from my own disease. The idea that we unknowingly shared the same fate made me suddenly feel like a brother to him. I asked the doctor whether he had attended that very clinic.

'I remember that patient – he suffered serious linguistic dissociation. Such pathologies are not uncommon among interpreters. Professional ethics prevent me from saying more; but your colleague refused to accept my care, clinging to crack-brained theories which were simply further confirmation of his illness. I don't know what happened to him in the end.' There was a brief silence. An evening mist was gathering over the lawns outside the window. Dr. Barnung was standing in front of me, thoughtfully rubbing his hands. I heard a brief rustling sound – the fabric of his stiff white coat – and the sound of rubber soles creaking over the parquet. Then the door opened suddenly, flooding the dim room with electric light from the waiting-room.

Leaving Dr. Barnung's language clinic, I found myself obsessed by the thought of the interpreter. I became more or less convinced that the disease from which I was suffering was a form of infectious madness, an illness that was endemic among interpreters, a lethal strain which would reshape and transform itself like influenza among the Chinese. Lacking sufficient linguistic defences, suffering from poor German and protected only by my French, I must have caught it from that man who was himself infected by a verminous pullulation of foreign languages. Unprotected by the antibodies of a thousand other grammars, for me such a disease might have effects that would be devastating. I started picturing linguistic infections and epidemics; my mouth felt like a breeding-ground for germs. I looked at the people in the airport waiting-room who were speaking foreign languages as though they were so many spreaders of the plague. And now I understood how the interpreter must have suffered when he saw his life crumbling under the blows dealt him by that wily illness which was destroying the most precious part of him, the well-honed instrument of his profession. He had tried to explain the phenomenon to himself as best he could, dreaming up far-fetched theories, seeking senseless explanations which had inevitably ended up by disconcerting and infuriating his superiors. Loneliness and fear had done the rest. I began to feel a desire to track him down, to apologise to him and make up for the harm I had unintentionally caused him by offering my help. I had become like him, we were dogged by the same ill-luck. But, by persuading him to put himself in Dr. Barnung's hands, I could still rescue him from the abyss of madness. In my dreams, as the cure progressed, I imagined a rare and open friendship growing up between us, nourished by gratitude, a lasting closeness which had no need of the complex underpinnings of love. Saving that luckless man would be my own redemption. But perhaps, at the same time, I realised that, by now, his company alone could afford me some relief, that his was the only presence I could still bear to have beside me.

In the weeks that followed, I too was obliged to give up work. The Personnel Department sent me before a medical tribunal, which coldly noted my impairment and left me no alternative. My heart strangely light, I saw documents piling up on my desk containing the same time-worn phrases as those which Stauber had drawn up in connection with the interpreter; but this time no one objected to signing them. Within a few days I had received notification of my dismissal for health reasons; my colleagues shot me sombre glances in the corridors and my secretary would lower her voice on the phone when I went into the office. Suddenly I no longer had anything to do; the pages of my diary remained blank and I spent my days in a state of suspended animation. My superiors summoned me to hear a farewell speech and receive an award, but I neither answered their invitation nor attended the event. For once, Irene would have been proud of me. I received a letter from the administration requiring me to remove my personal effects from my desk and cupboard by 5 o'clock by the afternoon of Wednesday 23rd Sept at the latest, to return my identity-badge to the Security Office and to take the parking permit off my windscreen. Felix Bellamy, grade one international functionary, destined for a brilliant career, had been wiped off the map.

Dr. Barnung's warning remained lodged in my mind, and I had now decided to put myself in his hands. I felt that the woes that had beset me were more important than my work and my career, that they spoke of a secret force which must be treated with the utmost respect and commitment. Before setting out for Munich, though, I was waiting for a sign, a time that seemed propitious: autumn, perhaps, season of mellow fruitfulness. I would lock myself up within the walls of Dr. Barnung's clinic as though in a monastery. Part of me sought such segregation, I was prepared to give myself wholeheartedly to the antiseptic practice of solitude. I told myself that I would be tempered by such spiritual gymnastics, it would make me stronger, better, more able to bear all that life still held in store for me. But, at the same time, I felt a growing desire to have news of the interpreter, to know what had become of him. From a more practical viewpoint, by now convinced that we had been struck down by the same malady, I hoped that by tracking him down I would gain a clearer idea of its course, alleviate its symptoms, perhaps even discover an antidote. Maybe he was already cured and could give me some advice; or maybe he had been entirely overwhelmed by it and was already imprisoned in a maze of incurable madness. Whatever his fate, it interested me.

With the help of a clerk who worked in the Personnel Department, I managed to get the interpreter's last address. I knew the road in question, it was in a modern part of the city near the station, where the buildings were mostly furnished flats rented by businessmen and adulterous husbands. The window of the interpreter's apartment looked out over a small square containing an unkempt garden, and it bore a notice with the words 'To Rent'. Feigning an interest, I knocked at the door of the porter's lodge to ask to visit it; puffing and panting, a woman took a set of keys off a hook and pointed to the lift.

'You'll see, it's a pigsty! He's left all his stuff there, and what a state it's in! They'd better get a move on and clear it out!' she grumbled, pressing the button to the third floor.

'I could tell from the start that he wasn't quite right in the head! I've got an eye for such things!' she said, waving her index finger around by way of warning.

'Of course I was younger in those days, and looked at men

more carefully,' she added, attempting a flirtatious gesture and lifting a hand to her hair while glancing in the mirror; then, clasping her hands behind her back, she lent against the wall and carried on:

'He's lived here for over twenty years! You might say that we grew old together but believe it or not, he never addressed a word to me. He'd talk to himself, or into a tape recorder, but never to another human soul!'

She glanced at me out of the corner of her eye.

'Anyone can talk to themselves, everyone has their troubles, as I myself know since my husband died. But what he did couldn't be described as talking! And at night, too! It sounded as if he were talking in his sleep! It must have been all the queer languages he knew; his head must have been churning like an upset stomach!' she added, putting on a smile.

The door, when it opened, did indeed reveal a monumental mess: piles of books on the floor, clothes draped all over the place, over the bedhead, on window handles and the dresser. The bookshelves, the worktop in the little kitchen and the windowsills were crowded with empty mineral water bottles, all of the same make, their green reflections visible on the walls; pairs of shoes, dozens of them, all English and all black, were lined up on the carpet.

'They'd better not think they can ask me to clean up this lot! They'll have to get the pest control people in first!' she protested, running her hands over her apron and looking around despairingly.

'And all this post! What's he hoping for? That we'll have it all sent on to him?' she went on, pointing to a pile of letters and periodicals on the floor.

'Didn't he leave an address?' I asked.

'Address my eye! He just went away, it must be four months

ago by now. And that was the last we saw of him!'

She made a quick tour of the room, then paused at the door to the bathroom.

'Well, do have a good look round and pull the door to behind you when you're done – I must go down, I've got something on the stove,' she said, and hobbled out on to the landing.

The first thing I noticed was the colour of the ink, then I recognised the handwriting. That particular shade of violet, veined with green, had been her nod in the direction of artistic caprice; together with her envelopes and writing paper, she'd had it specially made for her by a stationer's in the centre of town. It contained the juice of some poisonous berry, and if you drank it you might die.

'So it's true that words can kill!' she had commented, laughing, as she removed the wrapping paper from the little dark glass pot with the gilded label.

I bent down to pick up the envelope with Irene's unmistakable writing on it; I was afraid that I was seeing things. It suddenly seemed to me that I recognised the place. But when could I have been there before? Seized by a sudden feeling of dizziness, I knelt down on the carpet and ran my hands frenetically through the pile of post; rummaging through dusty periodicals and faded printed matter, I found two other envelopes bearing that same violet handwriting. My head was spinning, fury and fear were raging through my veins, taking my breath away. I was no nearer to understanding it, but at least I could now see what I'd failed to see for months. Irene, with that man! How could it be possible? I tore the envelopes open viciously: the first letter was dated 3rd May, the second 27th June and the third 20th July. I tried to turn on a lamp, but there was no power. I went up to the window where there was more light.

Dear Piotr,

I call you by that name because you cannot be anyone but Piotr, the Russian in the film the other evening. You translated it so well that that's how it must be. Are you really so melancholy? You're certainly every bit as enigmatic. Would you too hang yourself for so little? I do hope not. At least wait until the end of the season! Or perhaps you are Snorri, the Viking pirate from last Sunday's show? The one who never wanted to grow old, and went to have himself killed by his worst enemy. On second thoughts, you might be Yamada, the Japanese nihilist – what a wonderful film! Dark and cynical, and that's how I like them. But perhaps it was your voice that made it seem so marvellous – not only are you a simultaneous translator, you're also a true actor. How do you do it? How can you translate the characters' very souls? How can you give yourself over to them and then so quickly find yourself again? How do you always manage to pull yourself back from the brink of your excursions into others? And how wonderful it must be to speak so many languages! Truly, you have the sounds of the whole world in your head. Excuse me for this intrusive letter, it's not my style. But you left me a card with a telephone number that no one ever answers, so I had to write, and I hope to have better luck by post. I'd like to get to know you more, the couple of words we exchanged in the bar after the show were not enough. I want to know whether you are Piotr, Snorri or Yamada, but perhaps I will indeed have to wait for the end of the season to find out! Who knows how many other tortured characters you'll have played before the end of June!

Here's my address and phone number.
Get in touch!

Yours,
Irene
(The woman in the third row who always asks a lot of questions.)

I was sweating and my hands were shaking; a chill was slowly creeping into my bones, numbing my limbs. A door banged on the floor below, and a blast of cold air blew in from the stairwell; the clothes hanging from the bookcases fluttered, made a faint rustling sound. I crouched down in a corner, threw the letter on to the table and began to read the next one, the one dated June 27th.

My love,

If I may call you that – once again, I'm writing you a letter, for speaking no longer serves any purpose. I don't even know if you listen to me when I talk to you, or whether you've already flown away on the wings of your impenetrable thoughts. I don't understand what's happening to us. I know, it's my fault. It was all so wonderful, there was no need to say anything. We were so close, we both felt it; and that was enough, or rather so much more than enough. But I wanted to talk, to question you, to know and, by doing so, I ruined everything. Do try to understand: I know nothing about you, I don't know what you do on the other six days of the week. I don't know anything about your hopes, your dreams, whether you're happy or unhappy. I don't know what you think about when you're not with me. I feel that I have a substitute 'you' beside me, someone who resembles you but is not you. The real you will come later, and I and your substitute are here waiting for you and, as we're waiting, we don't know what to say. We look at each other, I smile at you, you tell me fascinating things about strange languages and our meetings are like television documentaries. When we say goodbye, when dusk falls on our afternoon ramblings around the city and I go homewards with a heavy heart, I keep my mind closed tightly as a fist, so that the precious treasure held within it – my rare time with you – cannot escape. Yet when I loosen it a bit, there's nothing there; you've flown away. I thought I had you in my grasp, but you weren't there at all. All that I know of you is what you've let me know: a shell, a voice. All that's left to me of you, when we part, is your voice. I feel alone; the air around me feels cold, there's an icy feeling in my house, in my life. You broadened my mind, made me see worlds I knew nothing of; whichever language you speak, your words enthrall. How could one resist the thousand visions that you conjure up before me, the imaginary worlds you set up and inhabit? But there is something false in you, and sometimes I feel that what you are giving me is not yours to give – that you have stolen it from someone and are giving it to me to rid yourself of it, as though it were some kind of proof that could implicate you in some crime. No sooner do I get some hint of you, manage to grasp something that seems authentically you in that shifting mind of yours, than you cast it off and proffer me the empty shell of what you were. I was looking for warmth, friendly affection; more, perhaps; I thought you too valued our Sunday afternoon walks. I thought you needed me, as I did you. But you have need of nothing, of no one, and you treat even yourself with strained detachment; as though you had become bored with yourself and were trying to get away, to slip out of your own head and occupy a new one – a whole new world to be discovered, filled. This is the last Sunday of the season; after that, we won't have any reason to see each other again, unless we seek it out ourselves. We'll nod to one another, and then I'll never see you again. But if you want me to stay, tell me so. With words – your own, for once, not those you pluck from others' mouths. Then all my days will become one of our magic Sundays.

I love you.
Irene.

A chasm opened up within me, and I plunged into a black magma which burned my vital organs without filling them. I was breathing from my throat, unable to open my lungs, paralysed by the sheer horrific vastness of my discovery. I tore open the third and last letter, the one dated 20th July, bearing a Zurich postmark.

My cruel friend,

Where have you gone? What has become of you? I've looked for you everywhere. You don't answer the phone; you're not at home, I've been by a thousand times and rung your bell, at every time of day. The concierge was starting to give me funny looks. There's never a light on in any of your windows; I sat outside in the car for one whole night, waiting to see when you'd get back, what you were doing. In the white light of the moon, I imagined rooms I'd never seen; it's only now, after two months of knowing you, that I realise you've never shown me your house. I even started to think that perhaps you didn't live there at all, that the card you'd given me wasn't even yours. I went to look for you at the *Étoile* Cinema but they didn't know anything about you either; at the sight of those dark red seats, my heart missed a beat. I asked the cinema manager to let me into the interpreting booths for a moment; in yours, I thought there was still a ghost of your smell. You'll say that that's impossible; it must be because I've still got it in my nostrils, and seeing places where I'd been with you just brought it back. I started to cry. The manager beckoned me to go down again, but I couldn't because I was crying, and when he noticed, he came up and closed the curtain.

Please, write to me, tell me where you are, just tell me that you're still alive, goddamit! You've got my address in Zurich, write to me there. I'll be leaving soon, I can't bear to stay in this city any more, it's been poisoned by unbearable memories; even the light of the changing times of day reminds me of you. So at two o'clock I'm in agony because you aren't meeting me in front of the station, at three because we're not strolling through the empty Sunday streets, just you and me, cars parked and cats on windowsills; and then again at four, when I can no longer see you but hear your voice in my head, your voice which speaks so many words, all the world's words, except for those I long to hear. What are you looking for? What ghost are you pursuing, what secret suffering has you on its hook? Or is it you who are in flight? From what, from whom? Are you a murderer who has left gruesome acts behind you? Why don't you tell me about them? Why have you never talked to me of yourself? It is only now that I realise that it's not you I am in love with, but the characters in the films that you translated: a different man each Sunday, because that's all you've ever given me of yourself. So now it's Piotr I'm in love with, perhaps because he was the first, laden with promise; and perhaps because he was the gentlest of them. But Piotr hung himself, poor bastard! And you're not here, you never have been, you've never existed! In which case, how shall I ever forget you? How can I wipe you out of my mind, you who are the sum of so many absences, the blank mirror in which I seek... you, who are nobody, and myself. And who can rid me of myself?

I shall love you for ever.
Irene.

Irene, my Irene slave to that madman! Now I understood those restless Sundays, the windy afternoons of that fateful spring when I would watch her preparing eagerly for her cinema matinées. I shouldn't have let her go alone, least of all to the foreign season. But who could have known, who could have possibly imagined... It was all so unbearable that I felt a sudden desire not to believe it. I might have been able to leave that room, go down into the road and cross the little garden as though I had discovered nothing. But those three letters in their yellow envelopes had put a stop to that; rather, what they did was to trigger off new suffering in me. That man was like a maelstrom, sucking anyone who approached him into its vortex; he had swallowed up Irene, inexorably dragging her away from me and then contaminating me too with his own vile evil.

I picked up the letters and stuffed them back into their envelopes, thrusting them into my pocket. Outside, the sky was now becoming covered with low threatening banks of cloud; inside, too, darkness was gathering, the first raindrops pattering on the dirty window panes. The lift started up, and a square of light fell on the table, revealing a thick layer of dust disturbed by the wanderings of my hands. I was on the point of leaving when my eye was caught by a piece of folded paper tucked beneath an ugly glass vase placed in the centre of the table. In the midst of such chaos, the table was the only surface which had been left unencumbered – except for that vase, with that bit of crumpled paper. I picked it up and unfolded it. It was a list, written in capitals, with the names of various far distant, scattered cities:

Vancouver
San Diego
Papeete
Vladivostok
Pusan
Taipei
Surabaya
Durban
Eilat
Constanta
Odessa
Klaipeda
Tallinn

Apart from Constanta, Odessa, Klaipeda and Tallinn, the others were all crossed out. I saw those places – so far away, so different – as tracing an unbroken line around the globe, thickening in the Far East and then again in Europe but leaving a vast gap between Surabaya and Durban. Then I realised that it must be an itinerary, some abstruse trail to be followed up. I imagined that, rather than heeding Dr. Barnung's warnings and placing himself in his hands, that man had ended up believing his own visions and had hurtled off to those far-flung places in search of the phantasmagorical language whose existence his madness had summoned into being. He had visited them one by one, striking them off his list; the only ones left to visit were Constanta, Odessa, Klaipeda and Tallinn. I remembered his study course: Romanian, Ukrainian, Lithuanian, Estonian, four of the few languages with which he was as yet unacquainted and which he had perhaps gone to seek out, following his own crack-brained theories. I imagined him drinking his fill of words which his famished mouth was learning to savour; at each new one he uttered, I saw his own appearance shifting, a kaleidoscope of masks. I was tempted to think that perhaps that man was one of many, that I had encountered just one, but that there were hundreds of others like him, pursuing one another, wandering round the globe, usurping voices and faces not their own, leaving a trail of old clothes, shoes and mineral water bottles strewn behind them, as in that flat: the indecipherable armoury of madness. I decided that I would root him out from wherever he was hiding: no longer to help him, or to pool our sufferings, but rather to witness the course and climax of his madness for myself. My heart full of glee, watching him as he gasped, racked by spasmodic seizures, I would tell him that soon all his languages would crumble away and dissolve into one rank mush. Secretly, though, I sensed that it was not just the poisonous desire for vengeance that was driving me towards him. No, something stronger was at work, something I was trying to hold in check within my mind: some frightening affinity, some inexplicable and voluntary attraction which I was trying to resist with all the strength that I could muster. I felt a physical need to sense him at my side, to hear his voice, to smell the bitter odour he gave out, as though he were at once cause and cure of all my woes.

Sensing that it was late, I shook off these thoughts; by lingering on such fantasies, I too was running the risk of going mad. The evil blossoming in the soft reaches of my mind might overwhelm me; if I wished to avoid the fate awaiting the interpreter, I would have to shuffle off such crazed wool-gathering; I would have to set about finding a cure and close up the dangerous wound which was cleaving me in twain.

Throwing a few clothes at random into a suitcase, I left one morning in late September. Heavy of heart, I looked back through the darkness at my house from a rise in the road. Would I ever be seeing it again? Would I ever go back to tend my roses, would I ever return to my old reassuring groove? At that moment, all seemed to be lost forever. The plane to Munich was almost empty; the autumn sun fell glancingly through the little windows and, as I slumped into my seat, I remembered the peaceful hours of distant afternoons, punctuated by the untroubled hum of radiators and warmed by the busy presence of Irene. I had the brief sensation that what I was embarking on was utterly absurd; that in reality my illness was pure fiction, that it had all been a passing frenzy brought on by loneliness. I was going to lock myself up among lunatics, I was putting myself into the hands of a neurologist who was eccentric to say the least, submitting myself to a course of treatment about which I knew precisely nothing. But suddenly, at that very moment, uncontrollable whistling and gurgling noises sprang from my mouth, truncated words pronounced in a voice which was not my own, while my neighbour looked at me in alarm, then hid his face behind his quivering newspaper. I wanted to

cry out, to call for help, to tell someone about the fearful ill
that was devouring me. I tried to catch the hostess's eye as
she passed by with the drinks trolley; she had strong hands
and her face was strangely lined, as though she had slept on
a rumpled sheet; her lips and eyelids were smeared with oily
make-up. She looked at me severely, as though she had noticed
my lapse and wanted to reproach me for it. For a moment, I
had the absolute conviction that I was part of some vast and
faultlessly-orchestrated set-up, that the hostess herself was a
nurse working for Dr. Barnung, deputed to work on this specific
plane and on no other; those hard eyes of hers, those gnarled
hands, those strange wrinkles were all designed to strike fear
into me, the kind of fear that renders animals docile as they are
herded into the abattoir. I drank my fruit juice obediently and
bent my head in resignation. I fell into sleep as though into a
swoon. In my dreams, Dr. Barnung was cackling, laying his
gnarled, clasped hands upon the table while, behind him, the
window overlooking the garden lit up with a strange glow.

'I see that you've settled for the wiser course!' he noted,
ushering me into his study. 'You'll see – you won't regret
your choice. This place is made for you; you'll soon be right
as rain.' At that moment, a thin woman came into the room,
wearing a long white coat revealing only forearms and calves
hairless as eggs; sheathed as it was in thin yellow stockings,
her skin had something sickly about it, and for me that colour
instantly became a smell – of a dried-up wound, an antiseptic
ointment. The woman gave me a slightly servile smile, like
that of maid to master, then gestured sharply towards the door
she had left half-open behind her.

Escorted by the nurse, I went down long white-painted
corridors where total silence reigned; a smell of the schoolroom

wafted from such few doors as had been left open, and I caught a glimpse of listening-stations shielded by insulating panels, with rows of headphones hanging from hooks. The floors were covered in soft linoleum which sank beneath my feet as I walked. We went up to the third floor and through a door bearing a notice with the words *Deutsche Abteilung*. My room gave on to an inner courtyard with a small square lawn crossed by little gravel paths; the furnishing was simple but carefully chosen, all in light wood. The nurse opened a cupboard door and handed me a set of sheets and towels; then, after looking me up and down, she started rummaging among the coathangers until she found a blue uniform which she then laid out on the bed, attaching a small strip of red material to the press-studs on the pocket.

'This is the uniform of the German section. You have to wear it during the therapy sessions, in the refectory and in all communal spaces,' she informed me.

'And what does that red strip on the pocket mean?' I asked, running my hands over the rough cotton uniform.

'It means that you're not allowed to speak French. No one must ever address you in that language, and you must never use it to communicate with the other patients. You'll find all the explanations you need in that handbook,' the woman told me, pointing to a booklet on the table.

'Supper is at seven. The German refectory is on the ground floor, at the end of corridor B,' she added, before closing the door behind her. Alone at last, I sat down and started leafing through the clinic handbook, a small volume with the text printed in German on shiny paper, interspersed with images of the clinic and surrounding park; the cover bore a photograph of the medical staff assembled in the courtyard. I recognised Dr. Barnung, sitting in the back row with his shirt unbuttoned, next to the nurse who had shown me to my room. A brief introduction explained the principles of linguistic therapy, following the line taken by Dr. Barnung when he had briefly explained it to me, but going into matters in greater depth. I now discovered that each language had a colour, as did the relevant treatment rooms, refectories and corridors. An index card with my name on it informed me that I was to present myself at the yellow laboratory – the one for Romanian – tomorrow morning at nine on the dot, and a map of the building showed me the route I would be taking to get there, also shown in yellow. The clinic made use of three languages for introductory purposes – German, French and Russian - and each such language had its own uniform – blue for German, red for French and green for Russian. These languages served as a sort of gymnastics, a warm-up for the muscles of the brain, but also to prepare the patients for the specific cure that they would undergo, and lastly as a sort of fixative, since their practice would reinforce the results obtained in the patients' minds by the therapeutic languages. These latter were much more numerous than the introductory ones, and furthermore they required periods of isolation when courses in languages defined as dangerous would be administered, marked by the colour white. I closed the handbook and looked out of the window. Darkness had fallen and the lights were on in many windows; torches were burning in the courtyard. I picked up my uniform from the bed, unbuttoned the tunic and put it on; looking at my reflection in the mirror, encased in the rough fabric of a garment that was only approximately my size, for the first time I felt truly ill.

Each patient had a numbered place in the refectory; my table was next to a large window overlooking the courtyard. My fellow-diners, four men and a woman, had already begun their meal.

'Welcome,' said my neighbour, rising to greet me.

'My name's Ortega,' he added, shaking my hand warmly. 'And may I introduce Mr. Vidmajer, Colonel Kwiatkowski, Mr. Vandekerkhove and Mrs. Popescu.' They greeted me with a nod. The oldest of the group, Colonel Kwiatkowski, lifted his eyes from his plate, dried his mouth carefully with his napkin and stared at me at some length; his face was a maze of wrinkles and his almost white eyes were scarcely visible beneath his fleshy eyelids. I noticed a whole thicket of coloured strips on his jacket pocket.

'Another one who mustn't speak French! So what's happening to all those French speakers out there?' he burst out in annoyance before dipping his spoon back into his soup.

Mr. Ortega smiled, to let me know that I shouldn't take the old colonel too seriously.

I too began to eat my soup in silence, exchanging friendly looks with my neighbour from time to time.

'By now, almost all the French speakers from the old continent are locked up in here!' commented Mr. Vandekerkhove after a pause, to general indifference. He had very short red hair, and it was hard to guess his age; his freckly face was creased into a permanent half-smile. He wore a pair of small, round glasses, which did not serve to correct any fault in his vision, but which his face quite simply could not have done without. Kwiatkowski shot him a nasty look which failed to upset his bovine calm. The clinking of cutlery gained the upper hand and mingled with the faint buzz which was coming from the other tables.

'What news of the big outside world?' Ortega asked me, raising his voice a little so that everyone could hear.

I shrugged, desperately casting around for something to say.

'Is it true that by now the only language spoken is English?' he asked me, his voice suddenly grave.

'Not quite…' I ventured.

'Well, I'm here because I can't learn it,' he admitted, twiddling with his fork.

'English is the language of cowards and queers,' broke in the colonel angrily from the other side of the table, causing Mrs. Popescu to jump and raise her hand to her chest in alarm.

'Never trust a language which is written one way and spoken in another! Filthy transvestites!' declared the former officer, flapping his napkin in front of him, to general dismay.

The nurse who was passing between the tables with the food trolley was about to intervene. Ortega shook his head and looked disapproving; then he carried on eating, waiting for Colonel Kwiatkowski to lower his head to his plate again.

'Which intensive course are you taking?' he asked me cautiously after a pause, covering his mouth with his napkin.

'Romanian. Actually, I haven't started yet. I have my first session tomorrow,' I said without much conviction.

'Romanian? That's odd! You're the first person I've ever met here who's doing an intensive course in Romanian. I didn't even know there was one!' remarked Ortega, pouring himself a glass of water.

'Romanian's for schizophrenia!' Kwiatkowski burst in, his mouth full, jabbing his forefinger at the yellow strip attached to his pocket alongside five others, one red, one green, one mauve, one orange and one blue.

'And a fat lot of good it did me! Indeed, now I'm not allowed even that! They'll end up by forbidding me German too. That way I won't be able to speak at all, and then I really will be cured!' He burst out into a noisy laugh, revealing toothless gums, only to be seized by an obstinate coughing fit which caused his face to go purple. Holding his napkin to his mouth, he looked around him, as though seeking approval from his fellow-diners, but they kept their eyes firmly on their plates. Seeing the nurse approaching, Kwiatkowski raised his hands in a gesture of surrender; his eyes were bright and the veins in his forehead were swelling like whips as the coughing fit died down.

'Frau Goldstein, don't look at me like that, you'll give me bad dreams! I won't say another word, I promise!' he added hoarsely in a tone of mock alarm. The nurse paused for a moment a few steps from our table, biting her lip in disapproval, then went back silently to her trolley.

After supper I followed Ortega into the common room; chess sets and playing-cards were laid out; people could listen to music or read books and newspapers. There was no sign of any language except German; even the music was exclusively by German composers. Lined up against the end wall were various armchairs, with sockets for headphones linked up to a stereophonic player. In front of a large window, what looked like normal social activity was under way.

Two generously proportioned women, eyes heavily made up, were playing rummy at a table at the end of the room, in front of a large bookshelf which occupied the whole of the left-hand wall, smiling cheerfully at one another and throwing down their cards as though they were flowers. Beside them on a three-legged table stood two large tankards containing a cloudy liquid from which, every so often, they took an unenthusiastic sip.

'Watered-down anise,' explained Ortega, intercepting my look. 'Mrs. Guzman is Argentinian, and Spanish is her mother tongue. Mrs. Mikhailov on the other hand is Bulgarian, but they are both doing an intensive course in Greek. In the outside world, they both used to be opera singers, and both suffered serious nervous breakdowns linked to the stress of live performance; as you can see from their crimson stripes, both are forbidden to speak Italian. Mikhailov isn't allowed to speak Russian either; they caught her singing an aria from *Boris Godunov* in the bath, so she was given two weeks of intensive Georgian by way of punishment. While she was away, Guzman carried on setting out the cards for their game of rummy as though her friend were with her in the room, but Frau Goldstein, ever the stickler, refused to serve two tankards of watered-down anise. Outside the laboratories, no one has ever heard them utter a word; it's as though they were completely dumb. Even their expressions are dazed and vacant; but if you creep up unnoticed, you'll hear them communicating with each other through operatic arias – with their mouths closed, so as not to arouse suspicion. Frau Goldstein has twigged their game and tries in vain to catch them by surprise; but placid and harmless as they look, those two are as fleet as hares. The moment she starts creeping up on them, they swallow up their song and give her an angelic smile. They are the only people in the clinic for whom music is forbidden!'

Staring at their resolutely closed mouths, I too was tempted for a moment to try and catch them at it, but my attention soon wandered, intrigued as I was by the novelty of my peculiar surroundings. The centre of the room was occupied by a large billiards table; two scrawny men, who almost looked like twins, were chalking up the tips of their cues, concentrating on the arrangement of the balls.

'The one on the right is Captain Lindqvist and the other is Vassilenko, a former Soviet obstacle race champion; they look as though they're related, but they met here for the first time, and they've become inseparable. Vassilenko is a very serious type, he's been doing an intensive course in Urdu and by now that's all he'll speak; you'll hear him swearing in Urdu when he misses a shot. There's really nothing wrong with Lindqvist, it's just old age; when he retired, his wife found she couldn't stand having him under her feet all day after so many years at sea, she just couldn't be doing with him any more, so she persuaded him to come here. He thinks he's in an officers' club and calls everyone by the rank which he himself thinks that they deserve; for instance, he has Kwiatowski down as a common sailor. Oddly enough, the colonel doesn't take offence. "You godless cowards! I'll sink the lot of you before you even get out of port!" he shouts at him every time they meet.'

Ortega had taken on the job of introducing me to my fellow inmates. Without the slightest hesitation, or the slightest fear of seeming to speak out of turn, with just a hint of malice, he told me what illnesses the other patients were suffering from. For a moment I was tempted to ask him about his own problem, about what bizarre mania held him in its thrall, but I didn't want to break the flow. After all, his information was useful to me, it helped me take my bearings *vis-à-vis* those eccentric sufferers who would be my companions for goodness knows how long. I stared in amusement at the fake twins as they in turn stared at the green baize, already curious as to the rank that the old captain would assign me when we became acquainted, but was disturbed to note the white strip buttoned on to Vassilenko's jacket pocket. Ortega and I walked past the big window and sat down at a table set slightly apart, away from the crowd of various gameplayers, who would occasionally break out into lively argument; nearby, Colonel Kwiatowski was playing chess on his own.

'Don't pay too much heed to the colonel, he isn't always that brusque; actually, he's the jolliest soul on our table, he's just a bit of a loudmouth. Tomorrow he won't even remember what he said last night. But today has been a difficult day for him: they've put him on an intensive course of Seroa, an extinct language once spoken in southern Africa. He'll be put into isolation if he doesn't improve. Seroa is a very archaic click-language – it has three different types of click. Dr. Barnung has recourse to such brutal expedients only in extreme cases. But, as you can see, Kwiatkowski has run through almost all his languages; he can't keep a grip on anything. He's gradually absenting himself from his own consciousness; the languages he speaks are eaten up by the gangrene caused by the disease. He comes of an ancient and noble Polish family which emigrated to Germany, where they spoke a different language every day in order to honour all the branches of the family: German on Mondays, Russian on Tuesdays, Swedish on Wednesdays, Romanian on Thursdays, Hungarian on Fridays, Czech on Saturdays and Polish only on Sundays. Kwiatkowski needs all these languages to stay alive. His identity is a seven-headed monster; but only one of them can live. Think of septuplets, seven different individuals all sharing the organs of a normal body; it's a bit as though the colonel's liver were in Germany, one lung in Sweden, the other in Romania, his eyes in Hungary and his heart in Poland. Dr. Barnung is trying to sever the colonel's consciousness from those parts of him that will simply not be able to survive and save at least one of all those identities.'

I was having trouble grasping the nature of this obscure malady which Ortega was outlining to me with such learned ease.

'But why does anything need to be done at all? At his age,

surely the colonel could be left in peace?' I asked, perplexed.

'Not really. Because it was with age that Kwiatkowski was beginning to give signs of mental imbalance – the first hints of some linguistic disorder, albeit apparently quite harmless. He was mixing up his words, talking an impenetrable language all his own. Then, four years ago, during a hunting party with some other NATO officers, he started shooting wildly at his fellow-hunters, shouting 'Surrender, bunch of queers!' in every language known to him – one English lord actually perished in the fray. Since then, he's been in here...'

I glanced in Kwiatkowski's direction: sitting bolt upright in front of the laid chessboard, he was twiddling a bishop between his fingers as though it were some delicate insect which had just alighted on his hand.

'The most difficult person at our table is undoubtedly the Belgian, Vandekerkhove. He just can't help himself; he ruins every conversation with ill-judged remarks, picking on insignificant details, and since no one pays any attention, he ends up talking to himself. But that's certainly to do with his illness,' Ortega confided *sotto voce*, eager to carry on, assured of my interest by my look of curiosity.

'Vandekerkhove is bilingual, but he can't distinguish French from Dutch: when he finds himself among French speakers he talks Dutch, and vice versa. His ego has learned to solve this problem by mimetic behaviour: unconsciously sensing that the language he's using is not the one that's needed, but incapable of putting things to rights, he translates one word after another as he talks, and the result is incomprehensible bluster. Dr. Barnung is trying to cure him with an intensive course in German, he's trying to ferry his identity to safety on the raft of an emergency language; only when Vandekerkhove's identity is secure will he be able to proceed to the reconstruction of his two native tongues. But it seems that he's resistant to this cure and is learning a bastardised German; you'll hear it when you talk to him. It's a German that's been translated from something else, but Dr. Barnung can't find out from what, not even with hypnosis! It seems that by now Vandekerkhove is translating from some buried language of his own, one that he doesn't even know he knows, and in which he takes refuge in moments of stress.'

'And what about the other one?' I asked my well-briefed informant, referring to the third member of our dining-room coterie, the one who had been sitting in silence to my left.

'Vidmajer? He's a Slovene who grew up in a German-speaking community deep in the Argentinian pampas. The first time he left home to do his military service, he lost the power of speech. I think that the cure that Dr. Barnung has devised for him is his last hope; he's doing an intensive course in Spanish, with German as back-up. But he's still as silent as the grave; all he can do is repeat the phrases on the beginners' tape, and they're not much help in civilised conversation!'

Ortega seemed gratified by my expressions of amazement; he lowered his eyes and stretched out in his armchair, clasping his hands over his stomach.

We sat in silence for a few minutes, watching the fake twins busying themselves around the billiard table; the card-players had quietened down, a cloud of purple smoke rising above their table.

The two opera singers were smiling at one another, putting their cards down with ceremonious little bows. Ortega picked up some newspapers, leafed through them distractedly and replaced them in the rack.

'May I offer you a digestif?' he asked me after a pause, summoning the waiter; I accepted his offer readily and drank to my hospitalisation in Dr. Barnung's clinic of linguistic therapeutics with a glass of Jagermeister.

I was the only patient doing an intensive course in Romanian. The following morning I went into the sun-filled laboratory, sat down in the front row and slipped on the headphones, while the nurse threaded up the spool.

'Just breathe normally – at first you'll just be listening, trying to give yourself over to the sounds. Then you can start repeating them, but only when you see the red light go on.' I did as I was told. I half-closed my eyes, and when at last I heard my own voice resonating, I hardly recognised it: those soft consonants, those lingering vowels startled me, took me out of myself. The session went on for two hours, and when it ended I felt as though I was awakening from a drugged sleep; I was breathless and exhausted. The nurse accompanied me back to my room, lowered the blinds and handed me a bottle of green liquid.

'Gargle with this for at least two minutes – it's sulphurated water. Then go to bed – what you need to do now is sleep. In the afternoon we'll have a session concentrating on breathing and intonation; I'll see you at six, in the gym, and that will be it, for today. Tomorrow we'll start on the supplementary German.'

I fell asleep instantly, and slept as I had not slept for months; I awoke thoroughly refreshed, my mind clear as a bell. At lunch, I was alone at table; the nurse told me that my companions had already eaten. Taking a couple of books from the library, I went back to my room, but fell asleep again. There were about a dozen of us in the gym, taking various preparatory language courses. I noticed someone wearing a red uniform and nodded in their direction, but the red strip on my own jacket pocket caused people to lower their eyes after initial interest. In unison, after the nurse, we repeated voiced consonants and more or less open vowels, and ended with an exercise in tone, based on a Chinese ideogram painted on a panel hanging from the ceiling. Those three syllables echoed inside my head throughout the night, and I awoke at dawn with the sensation that I had been engaged in non-stop sleep-talking.

There were others with me on the German course: Vidmajer, Mrs. Popescu and one of the fake twins. It was only on Tuesdays that I would meet up with Ortega, and here our exercises were less monotonous: we had to repeat prose passages or bits of rhyming verse which I ended up knowing by heart. After those first days in the laboratory, I also had several sessions of linguistic hypnosis, under the supervision of Dr. Barnung himself. He sat me down in a special studio with sound-proof walls, all painted black, with daylight filtering in through a skylight of frosted glass; three series of Altaic diphthongs were played through a loudspeaker, and I had to repeat them until I fell into a trance, then he stood behind me and questioned me in French. I never knew what he hoped to discover with those sessions, but each time he looked thoroughly satisfied with the result.

Six weeks went by in this way. Romanian was making some headway in my brain, and I also began active language sessions, when I had to answer a series of questions using the vocabulary I had memorised. I was now beginning to feel strangely serene; I saw learning Romanian as my salvation and, as things were going, salvation did indeed seem to be within my grasp. All that I had to do was speak, keep speaking, and allow my voice to lead the way. Just as Dr. Barnung had foreseen, words were carving out sure banks between which the juices of my brain could flow without mingling, the backward-flowing waters of distress and fear now far from the pure sources of my new-found thoughts. Right from the very first sessions, my crises became less frequent and ultimately almost ceased altogether, though I was still surprised by the occasional attack, particularly in the morning, when I woke up. 'That is when linguistic awareness drops its guard,' the doctor explained to me. 'Emerging from the night has always been a problem for man. In the void of sleep, consciousness loosens up, the ego loses its weight and rises through the air like a balloon, becoming reunited with the vague pulse from which it came; and at that moment all that keeps our paltry identity in place is a thin plastic film. That's why, when you wake up, the first thing you must do is speak; any language whatsoever, even French, will immediately restore your identity to you, sickly though it may be. Words, your own voice, which distinguishes you from a billion others, will pull the fragile bubble of your identity back down to earth like a stone.'

After these sessions, I would spend many hours in total solitude, and this too did me good. The solitude I experienced in Dr. Barnung's clinic was of a completely new kind. No longer was I wandering down dark galleries which I feared to explore; now I was borne through light-filled halls in which I found traces of an earlier consciousness. I visited rooms furnished for all the Felix Bellamys who had never elbowed their way into existence, but whom I carried within me, unformed, irresolute. I sank into visions not my own, which yet belonged to me, with a familiar aura to them; I rediscovered pains experienced and never completely dulled, a secret birthright of lives unfulfilled. In a word, in Dr. Barnung's language clinic I felt myself happily unwell, assured of total recovery. Glimpses of a new identity were opening up before me, burgeoning in secret in the furthest recesses of my mind; thanks to Romanian, it was becoming less shadowy, brushing gently up against my mind. The doctor warned me that I must be certain of having reached its furthest roots before I tried to eradicate it. But I could also choose to let it take my place, I could pour myself into it through the channel opened up by the Romanian language. After two months I was actively speaking the language of the unknown Felix Bellamy who was reawakening within me, and a shiver of fear and excitement ran through me when I thought of the day when I would have to choose which of the two to be.

III

My life in the clinic slipped by almost imperceptibly, my
anxieties pleasantly blunted by a serenity whose origins were
all too clear to me, and which did not in the least surprise me.
Everything in that place was the fruit of some form of artifice,
of some complex intellectual fabrication; I too felt myself to
be a concocted being, devoting myself to my illness as to some
vice which I had learned to cultivate with skill, and from which
I could derive the greatest pleasure, while fully aware that I
was proceeding down a path of creeping addiction, although to
what I could not say – perhaps simply to the architecture of the
place, so secluded, so much itself, more fitted to housing the
members of some orgiastic sect than a community of sufferers;
or perhaps to the intriguing company of such weird people,
prey to irrational machinations, morbidly devoted to their
sufferings, flaunting their traumas, however horrible, with
pride. Magnetic and awesome as he was, Dr. Barnung himself
held a secret attraction for me; indeed, his very presence in
the common room after supper filled all of us with excited
alarm. He rarely visited the various therapy departments, and

his appearance always caused something of a stir; one section would compete against another, talking up his visits, obsessed by interpreting their meaning. Fridays were particularly tense, because hypnosis sessions were held on Saturdays, and the doctor would pass amongst his patients with an air of gravity, like a priest among his acolytes, as though calling for concentration, dedication, a deep, sincere commitment to his healing powers. We acclaimed him wordlessly – all that we did was buzz with sheer excitement, clustering around him as he passed, expressing our mute submission. We were putting ourselves in his hands, giving ourselves over to his arcane knowledge, not in order that he might cure us, but so that he might help us to preserve, intact, the illnesses that he himself had entrusted to us. Delicate and fragile as rare plants, they grew within us, sucking away at our will; we did not yet know it, but gradually they would take on our features, replace us, and it would be we who would disappear, as unexpectedly as the burning of a fever, a tightness in the chest, a passing twinge.

Over those first weeks, I came to understand that illness makes people more corporeal; I felt myself to be all body, and looking at myself in the mirror, beneath the transparent film of my epidermis, I felt I could see my organs functioning – swollen glands, purplish in colour, hard bulbs, pockets containing something granular, unpleasant to the touch, veins turgid with dark juices – everything in me was visible. In the grid of my brain I could even follow the intricate course of my thoughts, their rapid flicker behind my eyes, brief flashes partially obscured by my brainpan.

Ortega had been right – Colonel Kwiatkowski was extremely warm-hearted, although eccentric. He took a shine to me and would ask me to join him after supper for a game of chess, although that was just a blind – what he really wanted to do was talk.

'Believe you me, Mr. Bellamy, you don't come here to be cured, but to wallow in your illness. Languages are not a cure, they are a drug! I knew a patient who was doing preparatory Russian, a green uniform, in a word, who learned five languages for no reason at all, and none of them Slavic! No, he learned Italian, German, Danish, Greek and English. Dr. Barnung had diagnosed maniacal psychosis, to be cured with an intensive course of Italian, with German as a support language, as usual. After having learned Italian to perfection, he could have been discharged, but he asked Dr. Barnung for a few sessions in Greek; to strengthen the basis of his Italian, he said. The others followed, and over time the cure became a drug. I myself haven't heard from him for months, but in the gym they're saying that he's managed to wangle himself an isolation course in Japanese! Clearly, a man like that is not interested in a cure!'

I listened to Kwiatkowski's stories in fascination and amusement, even when Ortega was standing behind him, shaking his head with a mournful smile. One evening the colonel suggested a stroll in the courtyard. To get rid of Ortega, he had involved him in a game of cards but had then slipped away, leaving his place to Vidmajer. It had just stopped raining; a cool breeze was blowing, scented with leaves, and Kwiatkowski's few hairs were rippling over his head, making him look even odder than ever; he walked with his usual martial bearing, his hands clasped behind his back, his chin thrust forwards. As soon as we were alone, though, in the crystalline evening light, he gave me an agitated look, his face a tissue of wrinkles in the glow of the torches.

'Mr. Bellamy, do you want to know how to drive Dr. Barnung mad? It'll take you a few weeks to learn the trick, but it's well worth it!' he whispered, the ghost of a snigger playing across his face.

I looked more closely at his mocking expression, moving nearer to him so that I could hear what he was saying.

'Take this – it's a tape in Esperanto,' he whispered, dropping a package done up with an elastic band into my tunic pocket.

'Listen to it every night before going to bed, for at least a fortnight, or until you've learned it by heart. When Dr. Barnung calls you to his study for the hypnosis session, repeat the beginning of the tape to yourself. There's a good chance that instead of answering his questions during the trance, what you'll come out with is the contents of this tape – you'll be able to tell by his face when you come round. Nothing irritates Dr. Barnung more than Esperanto; it upsets all his theories! Esperanto doesn't deal in the unconscious, it doesn't do identity. So there's nothing to cure! The moment there's no language, there's no mother; and those who don't know their mothers owe nothing to anyone. We'd all be happy if we spoke Esperanto; like stones, or flowers. We'd be freed of our mad desire to be different from one another, we wouldn't feel obliged to remember things; we wouldn't feel we had to change, to go along with the vile blackmailing of time! Imagine that!'

Naturally, I paid him no attention, but I was amused by the imaginative way in which his spirit of rebellion showed itself; his illness had become so slyly camouflaged as to become unassailable, defying Dr. Barnung's most unforgiving forms of cure, making light even of an intensive course in Seroa.

'The glottologist comes once a month, and then I have to do my exercises like a good boy. But Frau Goldstein doesn't know Seroa, so on every other Tuesday I can talk gibberish to my heart's content! I send her smacking kisses and other rude noises down the microphone, and she squints at me and frowns suspiciously. She knows I'm teasing her, but she feels there's always a remote possibility that my smackers might indeed be Seroan, as rendered in a refined medieval Lesotho accent!'

For all his cast-iron cheerfulness, though, I could tell that Kwiatkowski was suffering. At table on occasions he would seem to withdraw completely, as though he'd lost consciousness and all that remained of him was an automaton, staring into thin air with frightened eyes, hands trembling. On such occasions, we were supposed to call the nurse, but none of us felt like putting the colonel into Frau Goldstein's clutches; he'd be put into isolation, and we were all secretly convinced that that was the last thing he needed, so we'd carry on talking calmly among ourselves. Mrs. Popescu took it upon herself to make sure that he didn't tip over plates or drop cutlery during his absences, which might last several minutes. When at last he had shaken off the vice-like grip of whatever it was that was making mincemeat of his brain, Kwiatkowski would carry on sounding off in his ringing tones as though nothing had happened; but he knew that he had had an attack, and that we had protected him. Mrs. Popescu would whisper something into his ear in Polish, and he'd give us a mild, grateful look. A sort of solidarity had been established around our table; we would protect and help each other, or perhaps simply respect each other. No one tried to encourage the silent Vidmajer to speak; Kwiatkowski himself never tried to rile him, preferring to concentrate his fire on the stolid Ortega, who would take it all with a smile. Together we would handle Vandekerkhove's blackouts, waiting for them to pass of their own accord, and then we would answer his tortuous questions patiently. We all held Mrs. Popescu in high regard; she was very reserved and shy; strangely enough, she was the one person of whose illness Ortega had told me nothing, and I never had the courage to ask. Rather than suffering from any psychic ill, she seemed oppressed by some shadowy fear, remote by now, but which would sometimes loom up again and put her in a state of high alert; then she would become red in the face, and hot, as though from fever, her breathing would become laboured and she would look around her as though seeking someone. She hardly ever stayed on in the common room after supper, she would never join the group of patients who went to read in the library, though she would sometimes stop to talk to Mrs. Vukobrat, to drink a herbal tea or have a game of dominoes; and she never missed the Thursday-night piano recital, when she'd always sit in the front row, eager and attentive. The moment the music stopped, before the small audience had begun to rise to their feet, she would leave the room almost at a run. I'd noted the yellow strip on her jacket pocket indicating Romanian, and wondered what her problem could possibly be; like me, she was forbidden to speak her mother tongue. One afternoon I was resting in my room after my intensive German course, prior to attending a hypnosis session, when I heard a knock at the door; I thought it must be the nurse who would be taking me down to it, but it was too early. What I saw in the darkened corridor was in fact the delicate silhouette of Mrs. Popescu, gesturing to me fearfully to let her in.

'Forgive my intrusion!' she exclaimed in agitated German; I drew up a chair and told her to sit down.

'I know I shouldn't be doing this, and it certainly won't do me any good; but I'm at the end of my tether!'

She was twisting her hands as she looked at me, her knuckles positively white; I noticed that her fingers were unpleasantly yellow, her nails ridged with bony excrescences. Her breathing was laboured, broken by suppressed sighs, as though she were about to cry.

'Please, I beg of you, speak to me a little in Romanian!' she implored me, now really on the point of tears.

I sat down on the edge of the bed; I wasn't sure that I had heard her clearly.

'What do you want me to say?' I asked awkwardly.

'Whatever you like, but please, just let me hear some Romanian!' she insisted tearfully. Seated in the middle of the room, her hands clasped between her knees, her over-large tunic hanging loosely from her thin shoulders, she looked like someone awaiting sentence for some unknown crime.

I didn't know what to say; all that came to my mind were inconsequential phrases, woefully ill-judged trivialities. Machine-like, I began to recite a text on the human body which I had memorised a few days ago in the laboratory: 'The human body consists of the head, torso and limbs. The limbs, that is, the arms and legs, are known as the extremities. The head is home to the brain, the tympanum and many other delicate organs; on it we find the ears, the eyes, the nose and the buccal cavity, in which we find the tongue. We hear with our ears, see with our eyes, smell with our nose and taste with our tongue; so the seat of hearing is in our ears, the seat of sight is in our eyes, the seat of our sense of smell is in our noses and that of taste is in our tongue. Within our torso we find important organs such as the heart, lungs, liver, kidneys, stomach, and the large and small intestines. Our body also contains bones, muscles, veins and nerves. Through our veins runs the blood which bathes our body, starting from the heart and ultimately returning to it. We use our hands for the most varied activities; we use our legs to walk. The body may be either well or diseased; all parts of it may fall ill, be affected by one or more maladies.'

I stopped in mid-flow, struck by the absurdity of my performance. I had spoken as though I was reciting a prayer; in front of me, weeping silently, her shoulders shaking, Mrs. Popescu had covered her face with her hands. I didn't know what to do; I went to the tap and filled a glass of water, but she shook her head when I offered it to her and dried her eyes carefully with her handkerchief. Then she rose hurriedly, rearranged her hair and dabbed at her face with her fingertips.

'Thank you! You cannot imagine what good that has done me! I promise you it won't happen again.' She opened the door, peered cautiously into the corridor and hurried away.

That was how I made the acquaintance of Roxana Popescu, the woman who was to precipitate my renewed search for the interpreter, although I did not know as much at the time. When she came to sit down at table, I saw her in a new light. Looking embarrassed, she flashed me a quick, complicit smile, but avoided my gaze and didn't say a word to me throughout the meal; she would stare vacantly at each of her fellow-diners as they contributed to the conversation, but never at me. Nor did she seem to be taking in Vandekerkhove's rambling monologue on the aphrodisiac properties of the freshwater crayfish, although she heard him out to the bitter end, nodding at his every word, while the rest of us had already been engaged in discussion of another topic for quite some time. After supper, seeing her lingering in front of the bookshelves, I went up to her.

'How are you feeling, Mrs. Popescu?' She jumped, then turned as though she were about to move away; but when she did answer me, her voice was hard and detached.

'Better, thank you, even though what I did was a mistake. Please, let's say no more about it.'

'As you wish; but I must admit that I found your visit rather disturbing,' I found myself saying, slipping a volume out of the bookcase.

'Forgive me. It was a moment of weakness, nothing more, and let's leave matters there. I'm here to be cured, and I must try to avoid any further such silliness,' she said curtly, still not meeting my eye; then she hastily picked up a few books and moved off towards the corridor. Over the following days, however, she relented somewhat; she still looked alarmed and watchful when she came to sit down at table, continuing to peer around before she took her place, as though she were still expecting someone who always failed to turn up. But now she too joined in the conversation, and sometimes shot me a grateful if covert look; she seemed calmer. Occasionally I would glimpse the ghost of a smile playing over her usually unbending features, rising unbidden to her lips and lighting up her eyes before it was edged out by the shadow of some thought, some besetting worry, always the same one, I sensed. I tried to strike up a friendship with her, but although she was now more approachable, she continued to ward off close contact with all and sundry. If she was now more willing to stay on to chat with Mrs. Vukobrat after supper, as soon as I approached their table she would gather up her books and stand up to leave; at such moments I would see the signs of a faded beauty lingering beneath the slightly puffy pallor of her features, a strong face struggling to emerge from the ruins but then collapsing wretchedly into a tearful moue, her eyes misting over, her mouth becoming small and bitter.

'Leave her alone. Believe me, Roxana's interest in you

is not of the kind that you imagine,' Mrs. Vukobrat told me sharply one evening as we watched my sad friend hurry out into the corridor with the nervous lope of a tracked animal.

'I assure you, all I want from Mrs. Popescu is a bit of company,' I said firmly but mendaciously to the old woman as she sipped her herbal tea.

'Roxana has told me all about it!' exclaimed Mrs. Vukobrat, giving me a reproachful look; blushing foolishly, I backed off, embarrassed by the implication that I had tried to take advantage of a sick person and oblige her to satisfy my baser needs. What a misreading of the situation! All I had done was to respond to her entreaties and rattle off some gibberish in Romanian! I didn't like Mrs. Vukobrat; I was irritated by her interference in my relations with Roxana. Noting my animosity towards her, Ortega hastened to inform me of her problems: she was Croatian, from Voivodina, and she had survived a spell in a Serbian lager during the wars in Yugoslavia. During her long months of imprisonment, in order to bear the physical and psychic torture to which she was subjected, she had developed a sort of camouflage reaction: in a word, she had ended up by accepting the thesis put forward by her torturers. She convinced herself that being Croatian was the height of iniquity, that her Croatian identity should indeed be obliterated, dispatched with hatchet blows; she forgot her own language and learned that of her torturers, becoming Serbian in heart and soul. But once she returned to normal life, becoming aware that she had turned into the worst of her own enemies, speaking the language of her people's murderers and forgetting her own, she attempted suicide, hoping to kill the Serbian tumour which had swelled up within her, strangling the true Ivanka Vukobrat. In the language clinic she had been directed towards an intensive course of Maltese, the language par excellence most foreign to her among the Indo-European tongues; Dr. Barnung was using small doses of hypnosis to restore her to her own mother tongue, Croatian. But she was old, her mind had been rendered inflexible by the terrors of the lager, and hopes of a recovery were extremely remote. Hearing her story failed to make me feel any more kindly towards Mrs. Vukobrat, though after her reprimands I was nonetheless careful not to renew my approaches to Roxana. I remained courteous and friendly at table, always ready to engage in conversation should she show any desire to do so; but as soon as the fruit plates were cleared away and the vases of dried flowers replaced on the refectory tables, I would bid her a demure goodnight and leave her to a *tête-à-tête* with her old friend, without making the slightest attempt to intervene. She seemed relieved that I had withdrawn from the fray, and would give me what seemed to me a grateful look, which further convinced me that perhaps Mrs. Vukobrat had been right – she had no interest in me. I would go off to listen to Ortega's chatter, or listen to a little music, gazing up at the square of starry sky above the courtyard.

At the beginning of February we found the courtyard piled high with snow, its chill glow spreading into the rooms and reflecting the sun's light. The nights too were lighter now; from my bedroom I could see the moon sail by in the sky as though through the porthole of a spaceship, its oceans taking on the form of faces I seemed to recognise before falling into the cloudy embrace of sleep. I often woke up with the strange impression that I could hear voices, or some noise in the room, some distant shout that had made its way across the ether and had come to die within these walls. I even went as far as checking the cupboard and bathroom, rummaging around under the bed, without the faintest idea of what I was looking for. I ended up by thinking that all that light must have disturbed my sleep; I pulled the curtains to as best I could and stopped thinking about it. It was at that time that Kwiatkowski disappeared; he failed to turn up for supper for several evenings on end; then Frau Goldstein spilled the beans.

'He's had an attack; it's serious, he's got to do an intensive course in Seroan until further notice. Dr. Barnung even thinks he might have to be transferred to a psychiatric hospital,' she explained to us in hushed tones, then left the room. We'd seen the last of the colonel at table, and we all suffered from it; conversation languished, Ortega no longer had anyone to tangle with. Even Vidmajer would glance up from his plate and cast a bewildered look around the room; Vandekerkhove could no longer engage so satisfyingly in his ramblings; now he now longer had a foil, and he soon ran aground, repeating himself like a stuck gramophone record, stuttering over the last disordered words of a speech of which he'd lost the thread.

Roxana too missed Kwiatkowski; she had a blank look about her, though her air of habitual guardedness seemed less pronounced. But she was clearly more deeply troubled by something else, and I could not imagine what it was. She no longer went to chat with Mrs. Vukobrat after supper, no longer attended the Thursday recitals; she would rush up to her room without even saying goodbye to her friend, who would be waiting for her in her usual armchair with her glass of herbal tea steaming before her on the little table with its fussy doilies. Roxana, my mysterious friend, had changed beyond recognition: she no longer talked to me, not even at table, she scarcely glanced in my direction. Mrs. Vukobrat too was surprised by this development and would cast me inquiring

looks, to which I would respond nervously with a quick shake
of the head. Roxana even seemed to shun me when it came
to our therapeutic activities; each afternoon, at the end of the
intensive course in German, in order to avoid being alone
with me in the corridor, she would make some excuse to have
herself escorted back to her room by the nurse, looking at me
out of the corner of her eye as she crept off, as though afraid
that I might follow her. In the gym she always tried to find a
place as far from me as possible, and she was always the first
to leave and scuttle off when the bell rang.

Some time later though, it happened again, this time in the
early afternoon. I was asleep in my room after my intensive
course in Romanian when I heard a knock at the door. Roxana
came in, looking even more agitated than she had on the
previous occasion. I was on the point of pulling myself out of
bed – I was still half-asleep. I was having trouble focussing
and I was flailing around looking for something to pull myself
up with. But Roxana grabbed my wrists and pushed me back
on to the pillow; then she straightened up and gestured to me
to keep quiet; her lips were trembling.

'This time it's going to be me who does the talking!' she
informed me in Romanian, her eyes sparkling.

'Just get me talking, it doesn't matter what about! Ask me
boring questions, anything, just as long as you get me talking
in Romanian!' I didn't know what to say; my brain had clouded
over, my mouth felt gummy, my throat completely dry. There
was something absurd and unreal about her request.

'What... I mean, have you changed your mind?' I asked,
propping myself up clumsily on my elbows.

'I can't help myself – I need my language, do you hear? I
have to speak!' She seemed to relish every word she spoke,

savouring each sound until it died out on her lips.

'So, tell me about yourself. Where were you born? What did you do in life before coming here?'

'I was born in Constanta, on the Black Sea. Until a few months ago I was the director of the town aquarium, I dealt with fish, octopuses, molluscs; my speciality was the reproductive systems of crustaceans, I would rear dozens of them in little glass phials. At first they're like fragile little spiders which would fit on your fingertip. Did you know that a lobster grows a centimetre a year? My favourites are the blue variety – even lobsters may show signs of nobility. I was happy in my aquarium, perhaps a bit lonely, but I wasn't the only one. And then he came along...' She shivered slightly as she spoke, as though she knew that I would find those words disturbing.

I sat bolt upright, suddenly remembering the list of cities I'd found in the interpreter's apartment; Constanta was at the top of those that hadn't been crossed out.

'Constanta? And who is 'he'?' I asked, now more confused and troubled than ever by my strange visitor.

'No, that's enough! Now I have to stop. Speaking Romanian does me no good at all, it claws at my heart and leaves it bleeding. It... it makes me cry, as you can see. I can't go on like this. Dr. Barnung will put me into isolation. I'm sorry, you're so patient with me, and I'm so cruel and unfair to you'.

She burst out sobbing; broken, disarmed and vulnerable, she was proffering me all her pain. I would have liked to take her in my arms, to hold her close – not in the way that Mrs. Vukobrat imagined, but because I felt that we had something terrible in common, something most grand, something we could not name but which loomed over us ever more threateningly.

'I must go, I'm sorry if I've not behaved very well. This time, I assure you, it won't happen again!' And she ran off, leaving the door ajar. That evening there was no one at her place at table; Ortega told us that she had been put into isolation, with a week's intensive course in Navajo.

Those days brought me back to reality with a jolt: I suddenly remembered why I was there at all. I had the feeling I'd been wasting my time: once again I had the urgent feeling that I must track down the interpreter.

When she returned from isolation, Roxana seemed changed; she was quiet and self-absorbed, as though she were following some new line of thought. Her jacket pocket now bore the doom-laden white strip which meant linguistic isolation, but her expression bespoke a new-found peace. She no longer looked alarmed or hunted; rather, she seemed at last to have shaken off that obsessive sense of expectation by which she had previously been dogged. She nodded at me affably when she sat down at table; we kept our questions to ourselves, talking of trivialities, giving Vandekerkhove free rein to unburden himself of as much incoherent babble as he liked. After supper, and a brief goodnight to Mrs. Vukobrat who had come to ask her how she was, Roxana went straight back to her room. I waited for a few moments in the common room together with Ortega, then excused myself and ran to the women's corridor. I saw the light under her door, knocked and went in without waiting for any answer. Roxana was taking down her hair, and looking at me in the mirror.

'What is it?' she asked me brusquely in Romanian.

'That man. Who was that man?'

'I don't know who he was. It may seem strange, but he never did tell me his real name. It started as a game: each day he'd invent a different one. He used to come and visit the aquarium, then we started to meet each other on the beach.

Don't imagine I was a total ingenue. I'd been in love, I knew a thing or two; but he took something from me that no one else ever had. Oh, similar things had happened to me in the past, sometimes I went for months unable to visit certain parts of the city because they reminded me of some lost love, unable to hear a certain song because it would make me cry.

As a little girl, certain smells had the power to make me feel unbearably nostalgic; even today, the acrid smell of tar from newly-laid asphalt gives me gooseflesh – and only I know why. But with time I've learned to protect myself; now I know how to retrieve whatever gets burned in the pyre of my love. For instance, I know now that it's better always to fall in love in the same spot: placed on top of each other, memories don't have enough space to burn, they die without leaving any bad smell behind them, and all that is left of the pain is an empty shell. So I thought I'd be able to emerge from this befuddlement unscathed as I had from the rest. What could this man take from me that I hadn't already lost? How many others had I not already mourned, standing at sunset by the sea, wandering alone through the sunset-streaked sand of a September evening, or along the windswept roads in the winter, when snowy roofs stand out against the dark sky? But the one thing that had never been at stake was my language, and it was that that this man was studying – he already spoke it so well that he took it from me! Now every Romanian word I speak is a torment I inflict upon myself, but it's also a spark in whose glow I can glimpse the marvellous time when he and I shared one single tongue; and I can't shake off the false hope that such sparks might rekindle that fire. Instead, though, each time I sink to ever greater depths, and then it's a huge struggle to come back to the surface. But now that I'm here with my head just above water I feel the call of the abyss, pulling me down; and I no longer have even my language for salvation, I can't even call out my name, because he's taken it from me!'

Roxana burst into tears, then, proceeding from tears to fury, she began to tousle the hair she had just been so carefully combing. I gripped her firmly by the arm in an effort to restrain her, but she fought me off with surprising strength, and it was only when I let go of her and retreated towards the door that she quietened down. Throwing herself on the bed, she lay there motionless, her mouth quivering, looking up at the ceiling with bloodshot eyes. 'Did you know that the Navajo also speak with colours?' she carried on after a brief pause, her voice still hoarse from sobbing. 'Sounds have a colour, because according to the Navajo the world was born from four coloured clouds. Scholars have even coined a specific term for the Navajo's coloured sounds: they call them 'pigmemes', a combination of pigment and phoneme. So in Navajo, for instance, whiteness is masculine and blackness is feminine, because all things are born of black, and all return to this same blackness when they come to die.'

I drew a chair up to the bed and sat down, taking her hand.

'Please, calm down, just try to forget about all that; stop tormenting yourself. In fact, why don't we talk German?' I suggested.

'No, please... Let me speak just a little more Romanian. For me, this will be the last time.'

At the time, I did not know what Roxana meant by those words. She apologised for having fought me off so aggressively, but it was I who felt mortified at having yielded to her entreaties. I felt responsible for the sudden worsening of her condition, and for the intensive course in Navajo to which she had been subjected.

'Don't worry! A little Navajo has done me good,' she

reassured me with a smile. 'But I've got a question for you too: what makes you so interested in hearing about him?'

'I know him; he worked for me, but it would take too long to explain,' I answered evasively. It was then that I was suddenly seized with the fear that Irene too might have met the same end as Roxana, and might even now be locked up in some psychiatric clinic, victim of who knows what form of madness.

'Do you know where he ended up?' I asked, returning to the matter in hand.

'He was on his way to Odessa; I don't know what he was going to do there.'

'That's the second city on the list!'

'You too know about the list?'

'Yes. What does it mean?'

'That's something I've never been able to understand. He was always rewriting it – on tram tickets, on restaurant bills, on newspapers. He'd recite it aloud all the time, like a mantra.'

I waited until Roxana fell asleep before leaving her; there in the moonlight, her face at last looked serene. I went back to my room, found my bag on top of the cupboard and stuffed my things into it. I was lost in a maze of thoughts, and it was a long time before I fell asleep. The following morning I went to Dr. Barnung's study to take leave of him, and his clinic too. He received me without a word and had me sit down in the armchair in front of his massive desk; the bright sunlight lit up our faces, setting the little glass medicine cupboard at the end of the room ablaze as though it were a sacred reliquary. The cat was crouched as ever on the windowsill, licking its paws; a few snowdrops had pushed up through the soil in the garden.

'Mr. Bellamy, your cure is not yet complete. By interrupting it, you are jeopardising all that you've gained so far. The sense of security by which you are currently pervaded is purely illusory, it is due to the daily salvo of intensive courses you are undergoing – it is not, how should we put it, self-generating. The beneficial effect of intensive Romanian is not sufficiently strongly rooted within you, it cannot yet sway your character. As soon as you abandon the daily gymnastics which support it, your language will once again fall into disorder. You're courting trouble, Mr. Bellamy!'

His solemn tones rang out like a threat, and he looked me long and intensely in the eye.

I arrived in Odessa one dark night at the end of February; a freezing wind was blowing, sending the dry snow swirling around like dust, heaping it up along the runways and hurling it against the hangars and the parked cars in the ice-bound fields. I chose a hotel at random from among the leaflets in the airport hall, and got into the first taxi to hand. We drove through vast squares filled with snow-covered lawns, with dark stone monuments towering above them, then through the wide streets of the centre, where streetlamps shuddered in the wind, sending dark shadows over the crumbling stucco façades of the old palaces. My hotel, *The Krasnaya*, was described as overlooking the sea, but I could not make out any water when we arrived at a modern building set somewhat back from the road. I found myself in a cold, ill-lit foyer, draped with heavy purple hangings; a few couples were sitting in armchairs in the bar. To the other side of the glass partition, a waiter was laying the tables in the restaurant; the clock above the reception desk was chiming eleven. A smell of deodorant sprayed over musty fabric filled the air. I saw that that evening I would be eating alone, with no one else to talk to, and I suddenly felt nostalgic for Dr. Barnung's clinic and for my table of eccentric fellow-patients. I would have preferred to talk to Vandekerkhove rather than endure that solitude. What I now saw before me was no longer the smiling vision of a life to come, but once again a yawning chasm, splitting off into a thousand narrow galleries. I realised that Dr. Barnung had been right: I was not cured and, once away from the Romanian laboratory, my wound was beginning to bleed again. I was seized by a sense of panic and struggled to prevent myself crying out; I felt suddenly powerless, rooted to the spot, paralysed by the expanse of time that was opening up before me like some foul intestine. I went into my room without even turning the light on, in order not to see the table in front of the window, the cupboard and the chair and the bedcover of dismal printed cotton. I lay down on the bed and tried to sleep but after a bit, to my total consternation, I was seized by a convulsion, the first I'd suffered for a long time. I leapt to my feet, trying to contain myself, taking deep breaths to lessen the spasms; but the usual senseless words, the usual mangled sounds gurgled up from the diseased depths of my being like a tainted wave, and all I could do was spit them out. When at last the attack was over I lay down again, weary and dazed; I wrapped myself up in the clammy covers and fell asleep. Over the days that followed, things got worse: the rhythm of my linguistic ravings quickened, and sometimes I would fall prey to strange dizzy spells. Infinite anguish was raining down upon me from measureless heights.

Despite my malaise, I persisted in my search for the interpreter, though I had not the faintest idea of where he might be, and faced with that boundless city I began to lose heart; my legs felt heavy, my heart sank like a stone. Yet somehow I felt that my man was not far away, and that sensation quickened my impatience, excited my already frayed nerves; bereft of Dr.

Barnung's beneficial mumbo-jumbo, I felt that only with the interpreter would I find relief. I could scent his presence in the air; sometimes I thought I saw his face in the crowded streets. Some irresistible force was driving me on and, against all reason, I yielded willingly to its call. Within me, someone who was no longer me, but not yet someone else, wanted to know where that man had ended up, and was using my body to achieve his aim, but Dr. Barnung's tapes were no longer there to keep him at bay. Sometimes, within me, I felt that the metamorphosis was actually taking place, I felt that 'other' surfacing under my skin; I would touch my face and find shapes I didn't recognise, sudden wrinkles and lumps I hadn't felt before, but when I ran to look at myself in the mirror I would find my face unchanged, merely alarmed by those inexplicable hallucinations.

I proffered a few banknotes to the hotel porter, asking him to let me check the register for the last few months, to see whether the interpreter had been staying there; aware that I was looking for a needle in a haystack, I nonetheless scrutinised the pages back as far as last July – perhaps he had been travelling under a false name, there was no knowing what documents he'd used. Then it occurred to me to ask the porter if he remembered any client who resembled him; but I found him impossible to describe, not a single feature of his face had lodged itself in my mind. Furthermore, whatever language could I say he spoke? I went systematically through all the hotels in the city, paying lordly tips to get my hands on the registers, but I found nothing. I would spend whole afternoons observing the comings and goings of taxi-drivers, self-serving busybodies in pursuit of powerful businessmen, women with showy jewelry perched on huge suitcases; I would listen to them talking, stare at their mouths without understanding a word they said. I thought of the interpreter, who could take possession of any language in no time at all, speak it like an impostor, as though it were his own. And I knew he didn't just learn them, repeating them and imitating their forms – he sucked them into his monstrous memory, pillaged them as bees do flowers, leaving them apparently intact but in fact drained of all blood. I thought of Irene, bewitched by who knows what words and lost forever; of Roxana, bereft of her mother tongue, prisoner of a silence which was destroying her mind. In my pursuit of the interpreter, I was running the same risks. I saw that he took something away from each language he learned, some vital quintessence which his greed snuffed out for good; that the voice of whole peoples was being muffled, deadened at his passing, their languages impoverished and castrated, and that the whole world was now scored by an invisible trail of silence which that diabolical being was covertly digging out ever more deeply with his unwholesome wanderings.

I would go back to my hotel before darkness fell, have an early supper and spend the rest of the evening in the bar, to ensure being dead drunk by the time I went to bed.

Had it not been for my loneliness and ill health, when I got on and off the buses or walked along the seafront I might have thought myself on holiday. I found a bus route which went out of the city to a nearby tourist spot on the sea, where I would spend whole days in relative tranquillity; I'd found the wreck of an old ship beached in the sand, and I would climb up on to the deck. Water had seeped into the seaweed-covered hull, and huge dark fishes had become trapped there; misshapen silhouettes, they swum around slowly, open-mouthed, drinking in the water as though nourishing themselves on the rusty metal as it dissolved. Leaning over, I could see their slimy backs, their bellies with their greenish scales. I would prod at them with a stick, trying to lure them out of their lairs, but the frightened creatures would simply dart down into the depths, leaving just the odd slow-moving bubble behind them. I felt strangely drawn to that grisly wreck, with its sharp smell of corroding iron; once there, I would lose myself in the wild seascape, offer my face to the carefree wind coming from the open sea as though it might purify me, heal my inner wounds, set me free from that dogged pursuit; or perhaps just sweep me away, like a bit of dry seaweed, like a cuttlefish bone. That sweep of blue, bitingly cold though it was, distracted my haunted mind and made me feel less alone; I walked along stark white beaches, thrashed by violent waves, disturbing fishermen and shell collectors, followed at a distance by a barking dog, for all the world as though it were one of those Sunday afternoons when I would stroll around the lake in former times and, lost in my thoughts, would walk so far that I would have to find a taxi to take me back.

One Sunday I went back to the city earlier than usual; the sky had turned leaden, and a sharp east wind was blowing branches and rubbish up on to the beach. Soon it began to snow; the frozen flakes mingled with the sand, whistling among the brushwood; I sought refuge in the bus, which was waiting at the bus stop. The driver was asleep and was not best pleased when I knocked on the door to ask him to let me in. The city, when we reached it, was sunk in snow, the whiteness of the streets marred only by the odd tyre mark; I went back to the hotel but hesitated to go up to my room for fear of loneliness. At least there were people in the foyer, the waiters were chatting to each other and a group had just gathered in the bar, drinking beer and laughing uproariously;

I lingered among the armchairs, uncertain as to what to do, when I found myself in front of a man wearing a sailor's cap, holding out a strip of cardboard bearing the words 'Stauber – Geneva'. I stared at it, intrigued by the coincidence. The man came up to me.

'Are you Gunther Stauber, the interpreter?' he asked me in strongly accented French. I jumped, then looked around me in alarm.

'That's me!' I replied firmly, without any idea as to what prompted this reply.

'They're waiting for you down at the harbour; after you've seen them, I'll bring you back to the hotel,' the sailor said, leading the way. We got into a car and made our way towards an outlying part of town strewn with abandoned antenna towers, half-built hangars and ugly, peeling blocks of flats; piles of snow were building up in odd corners and blinding slivers of ice hung over the drains at the edges of the pavement. Then, at the end of the road, the sea came into view, dark, rough and flecked with foam. The sailor led me to a pier where a French merchant ship was berthed, the Saint-Nazaire ; an officer came towards me from the deck and took me into the control room, out of the wind. We shook hands.

'Welcome on board, Mr. Stauber. I am Delattre, Captain Jacques Delattre. Above all, first I would like to thank you for agreeing to come to our aid. I must admit, when I first turned to the Red Cross, I wasn't at all hopeful; conditions being what they are, I couldn't see what they could do. But I've known Admiral Van Wijlen since naval college; we haven't often met in recent years, but we've stayed in contact. He promised me he would take a personal interest in the matter, and he's always been a man of his word. He'd spoken to me on the phone about a well-known interpreter, a top-grade functionary in some important Geneva-based international organisation and an expert in Asiatic languages whom he knew personally. A little less than a week ago, he cabled me to tell me that he had been transferred to Odessa. I'm happy to have you among us; even if, at this juncture, I'm not sure that even an expert like yourself can be of much use to us!'

Without the faintest idea of what he was talking about, I nodded, beginning to fear that I had got myself into something of a pickle.

'I don't know if you are *au courant*,' he said, clasping his hands behind his back and glancing at the sailor, who shook his head.

'I'm not *au courant* with anything; I only knew that someone from the Saint-Nazaire would be getting in touch with me,' I lied.

'Well then, let's go downstairs,' the Frenchman said, following the sailor to the companionway.

'You see, it's a strange business, one to be handled with care – we might find ourselves in trouble with the Ukrainian authorities. But it isn't an isolated phenomenon, either,' he went on as we walked. We came to a corridor lit by small lights screwed into the ceiling, then stopped in front of a cabin door.

'They've put him in here for the moment, but we found him in the hold where the timber is stored. He looked more animal than human – he was wearing just a filthy overall and his feet were bound up in rags tied up with wire. The nurse has given him a tranquiliser, so he may be a bit confused. We tried asking him who he was, but he just answered in that incomprehensible gibberish of his, and that was when I called in Van Wiljen – we need someone who knows the languages spoken in Siberia, which is where we imagine this man comes from. We ply a route between Nahodka and Marseilles, taking machinery to

Siberia and coming back through south-east Asia laden with tropical timber, calling in at Odessa where we sell some of our teak, and that's where we discovered him. But Nahodka is the only place where he could have come on board.'

The captain gave me a serious look and placed his hands on the handle of the cabin door.

'The worrying thing about all this, you see, is that he's the fourth man we have found in our hold in as many months; it can't be pure coincidence. We want to know who these individuals are, where they come from and what they are looking for on our ship; perhaps they are being sent by someone; perhaps, without knowing it, we're being made a third party in some illicit trafficking,' he added before sharply turning the handle of the cabin door.

The midget of a man lying on a camp-bed, in the glare of a neon strip, had eastern features and a mad look in his eyes; upon our entry he shook his head and gave us a wide-eyed stare. The captain and the sailor shuffled towards the back of the cabin and waited for me to speak. I would have to enter into the spirit of the thing and come up with some fabrication, so I addressed some words of gibberish to him, surprised by the ease with which I did so. Hearing my words, he frowned; I came out with another string of nonsense, which might have approximated to a run-down of my stay in Dr. Barnung's clinic: fragments of the Esperanto text which Kwiatkowski had tried to have me learn, something of what I could remember of Seroa, a bit of Navajo and Captain Vassilnenko's Urdu. Behind my back, the captain and the sailor listened in awed silence. After observing me at length, the man sat up, licked his lips, opened his mouth and began to speak. Then it was my turn to be dumbfounded: for a moment, I thought that it was the interpreter that I was dealing with. The man began to whistle and whimper and quack in just the same way as the interpreter had done, emptying his lungs to emit volleys of clicking sounds, then whistling again, but from his throat, modulating the sound until finally it became one heartfelt, pleading wail. Then he fell silent and lay down again, gazing at the ceiling with blank, staring eyes; at that moment some mysterious inner power took possession of my breathing and I too began to whistle, whimper and quack in precisely the same way as he himself had done, noting, even as I did so, that my rantings were strangely like his own. The whole thing lasted just a few seconds. Now the madman was looking at me, and he seemed suddenly to have become more aware of his surroundings; he began to bang his head on the pillow, twisting it from side to side, howling and clutching the bedframe with his hands. The sailor rushed up to the bed, slipped a leather thong around his torso and pinned him down, then used another to immobilise his legs; he took a syringe from a case he had in his pocket and injected the contents of a yellowish phial into a vein; the man soon quietened down.

The captain slipped out of the cabin and gestured to me to do likewise.

'Did you manage to catch anything?' he asked me anxiously.

'I must admit, I didn't. I don't know his language – if language is the word. I tried speaking to him in Tungusic and asked him a few questions in Urdu, but he didn't seem to react. Perhaps he's just deranged,' I added airily, amazed at my own cool-headedness.

'Yes, just like the other three! I too am beginning to think that this isn't some foreign language, just simple madness. It's rather alarming to think that all the madmen of Siberia have got their eye on my ship!' Delattre agreed with a worried frown.

'Yet it did seem to me that he responded to your last, er, what shall we call it, contribution – at least after a fashion,' he went on, clearly alluding to my attack, which he had taken as an attempt at communication.

'No, I don't think so; I think all I did was to frighten him even more,' I said, inwardly praying that I wouldn't be seized by another crisis.

'Why don't you go to the police?' I then suggested.

'Are you joking? We wouldn't be able to weigh anchor for weeks!'.

'What do you intend to do with this man?' I asked.

'I'll leave that to Janos – he dealt with the other three!' the captain said, pointing towards the sailor who was closing the cabin door.

I shot Delattre a horrified look, but he burst out laughing.

'Come now, what can you be thinking of? We don't throw them overboard! There are some nuns nearby who take such people in, and we keep them in business!' he reassured me cheerily.

'As soon as the sedative has worn off, Janos will put him in the car and take him to the nuns. We're setting sail tomorrow, so we're going to have to get rid of him before the day is out,' he added in a low voice, giving the sailor an expectant look, which was answered with a shake of the head.

The captain asked me whether I would care for a cup of tea in the control room before I left.

'My dear Stauber, a sailor's life is a complicated one! Think of us as a piece of France which is plying the high seas, and everything which happens to us, even the most trivial incident, has to be seen in that light; often it's France herself who goes on the attack. This business will certainly come to the ears of the secret services, indeed I happen to know that the French ambassador has already been alerted. Come to think of it, what are you doing here in Odessa?' he asked me politely as he refilled my cup.

'Oh, just the usual – updating myself linguistically, attending boring specialist meetings!' I ad-libbed blithely, sipping my tea and wishing heartily I could be out of there.

'How wonderful to know so many languages and to be able to understand the people you come across! Whereas I'm always cooped up in my cabin, travelling the world without seeing it. Imagine – by now I recognise the ports by the colour of the containers on the wharves! But I won't bore you with my moaning; I'll call Janos to take you back to your hotel, you could probably do with some rest.'

He rose and shook me warmly by the hand.

'One last thing,' I said before going up on deck. 'Could I go with your sailor to the convent? You see, if what your stowaway is speaking is indeed a language, I'd be most interested to know more about it; as a professional linguist, I'd like to see these other men who speak it.'

'Of course, Mr. Stauber! Indeed, if you do learn something, I too would like to hear about it. Janos will be happy to take you there; he's not actually one of our sailors – I'd describe him as an invaluable Man Friday whom we happen to have here in Odessa.' Delattre rose from the table and went off to summon his dogsbody.

We left the port in complete darkness; the wind had driven off such powdery snow as had remained on the quays, and now there was nothing to lighten the pitch-black of the night. The dark water tugged at the boulders with an oily sucking sound. After driving through the container port and leaving the last cranes behind us, we turned off the main route taken by the lorries and drove along a wide dark road which lead into the outskirts of the city.

Janos stopped in front of a white building with high windows. Stretched out on the back seat, his wrists held firm by lengths of adhesive tape, the stowaway did not utter a word during the entire trip; every so often I would turn around to catch a glimpse of his wild, staring eyes. We lifted him out and walked him into a sumptuous entrance hall smelling of must and urine; the sailor pressed a switch, and two weak bulbs in the wall lit up the gloom, revealing the steps of a wide marble staircase leading up into the darkness, flanked by a blackened balustrade. Beneath it was a wrought-iron gate leading to an inner courtyard. We ventured along an ill-lit portico and came to a sort of porter's lodge, from which a grey-clad nun emerged and came limping towards us; Janos said something to her, she glanced at me over thick spectacles and gave a suspicious nod. Two other nuns appeared and took charge of the stowaway, freeing his hands and leading him into an adjacent room; Janos and I followed the nun with the glasses. After going back through the stinking hallway, we went up the stairs to the first floor; the nun opened a door with a large key and we were greeted by a powerful stench of stale air and excrement. Beyond the door, without either windows or furniture, lit by a neon strip, was a large room, peopled by some fifteen men, leaning against the walls or stretched out on the floor, their eyes fixed on a large skylight affording a view of a grimy, green-flecked night sky. Their grey uniforms put me in mind of Dr. Barnung's clinic. The nun stopped us in our tracks, gesturing to us not to go any nearer to them; she whispered something to Janos, who translated:

'Soon one of them will start singing!'

The men had all turned to stare in our direction, silent and motionless. The first one to start was the one who had been lying on the ground; he opened his arms and let out a long whistle, then craned his neck and gobbled like a turkey. Everyone else then did the same, in one great burst of whistling, wailing and arm-waving, their eyes wide, their mouths forming little round holes before they began their cry. Then, apart from the odd squawk, they became silent and motionless once more; those who had been lying down lay down again, the others turned their backs on us and ignored us. The nun opened the door and preceded us down the stairs; once in the entrance hall, she again whispered something in Janos' ear.

'She says two new ones arrived last week, found on the road by lorry drivers. We don't know where they come from, nor what brings them here; they look Russian, or perhaps Mongolian, but we can't be sure,' said the sailor, translating the nun's words; the nun crossed herself.

'Ask her if I can see the new arrivals.'

After hearing Janos' translation the nun nodded and took us back to the porter's lodge, then to the sickroom where the stowaway from the Saint-Nazaire had been taken, together with two other men lying on camp-beds, one of whom was asleep, snoring noisily, his mouth agape, his head done up in a bandage with blood seeping through the gauze. The third man was seated on the edge of his bed with his back to the door, rocking incessantly, his head bowed. I went up to him: amidst the mass of tousled hair I recognised the wrinkled face of none other than Colonel Kwiatkowski. I called him loudly by his name and he stared at me; for a moment I thought he recognised me, but then I realised that his eyes were utterly blank. He half-opened his mouth and uttered a weary moan before returning to his rocking.

It was pitch-dark by the time Janos took me back to the Krasnaya; we made the return trip in complete silence. Finding Kwiatkowski among the whistling madmen had thoroughly shaken me.

'Don't hesitate to contact me should you need to,' said the sailor as I was getting out of the car. 'I'm always at the place where they land timber, wharf 13. Just ask for Janos, they all know me.' I nodded my thanks and stared after the rear lights as the car drove off.

The hotel porter was dozing in an armchair in the foyer, still dazed with sleep as he came to let me in.

'I'm sorry, I'd like to know whether Mr. Gunther Stauber has arrived,' I asked him while waiting for the lift. Yawning, the porter opened the register and leafed through a couple of pages.

'Yes, he arrived yesterday morning. Would you like me to leave a message?'

'No, no, it doesn't matter,' I said hastily, closing the door to the lift.

That night, although I was dead-tired, I could not sleep; now I knew where the patients referred to isolation therapy in Dr. Barnung's clinic ended up; the thought that that might also have been my final destination sent a shudder down my spine. I did not know that another destiny entirely, a far more subtle fate, was awaiting me far from Odessa. I was beginning to fear that I too had been one of Dr. Barnung's guinea pigs; I saw now that there was no alter ego to be eradicated from my consciousness, no unconscious understudy for Felix Bellamy to be brought back to life by means of an intensive course in Romanian, of all things. Infected by the interpreter, poisoned by the attentions of a criminal German neurologist, I too had been in danger of ending up as a whistling madman. I decided to return to Munich as soon as possible, to discover what was really going on in Dr. Barnung's clinic, of what monstrous experiment I had been the object; if indeed there was any antidote to the hideous cocktail of mental illnesses which had been implanted in my brain, that was the place to find it. But first I had to find out how Gunther Stauber was involved, and what the head of the German department was doing over two thousand kilometres from his interpreter's booth.

It was almost dawn when I at last fell asleep, to be awakened by the sound of the wind against the windowpanes; the sky was aswirl with a jumble of white clouds, and the city below seemed to be carved out of glass. Beyond the inlet, the sea was roiling, white with spray. I looked at the clock and saw that it was late; I threw on my clothes and rushed downstairs. Stauber had already left, but I was told that he was in room 314. At first I thought that I would wait for him in the hotel, but my impatience got the better of me and I went out into the city, in the mad hope of tracking him down. I hailed a taxi and had myself driven to the centre of town, seeking out ministries, museums and monuments, following the few tourists hardy enough to pause to take photographs. I took refuge in a bar to have something to eat, then wandered along the seafront to the ferry port. There, battered by the wind as I idly watched the queue of vehicles moving sluggishly into the hold, my eye was caught by a banner hanging from the façade of a building with large windows: 'XIVth International Congress on Cetology', it proclaimed. The conference centre – why had I not thought of it earlier? I ran up the marble steps and into the foyer. The sight of the standards hanging from their brass poles, of the delegates scurrying to and fro with their briefcases under their arms, the ushers in their grey uniforms with their bundles of leaflets, everything reminded me of my former post, of the dry-as-dust labours to which I had devoted so many years of my life. I looked around for the accreditation desk, then showed my passport to the usher, who looked me up and down suspiciously; he had a vaguely Asiatic air to him – close-cropped hair and narrow eyes, prominent cheekbones. He leafed through a register, said something in a low voice to a colleague, then turned to me:

'I'm sorry, sir, but your name does not appear to figure on the guest list; in any case, the congress is virtually over, the president is making the closing speech.'

'Never mind. I'd like you to register me and provide me with earphones for the simultaneous translation. You can see from my passport that I used to work as a high-ranking functionary for an international organisation,' was my firm but calm reply.

The usher balanced his cigarette on the edge of a brimming ashtray and looked enquiringly at his colleague, who shrugged his shoulders, taking refuge behind his computer screen. Blowing the smoke out through his nostrils, the usher made an impatient gesture, but then took my passport and copied the details into a register. He took a blue folder from a cardboard box and thrust it in my direction, together with a map of the city, a pass, a set of headphones for the simultaneous translation and a form for me to sign. I thanked him curtly, deposited my coat in the cloakroom and walked towards the red velvet curtain behind which lay the conference hall, which turned out to be full of bald heads listening to the president's speech. Standing on the stage, in front of a gigantic image of a nineteenth-century print of a whale-hunt, a small bespectacled man was waving his arms and reading out from a hefty tome. I sat down in the first free place I could find and, feigning interest, placed the blue folder on the little table attached to the arm of my seat and opened it up. In fact, of course, what really interested me was the simultaneous translation; I had seen the booths as I came in, high up at the back of the hall; I put on the headphones and began to twiddle the knob carefully until I hit upon the German translation, and heard Stauber's voice.

I leapt to my feet: so it really was him. I slipped through the hall, my eyes glued to the booth window. Despite the glass, I could make out the ruddy face of the head of department, who clearly recognised me and pulled back in alarm. Headphones still clamped to my ears, I rushed from the auditorium, jostling angry scientists who were taking notes with their expensive pens. When I reached the foyer, I looked for the entrance to the booths, but my way was blocked by a wooden screen; the place was too crowded for me to climb over it without being noticed, so I went towards the main entrance, hoping to find another route. At the end of a long red cordon, two guards bristling with serious-looking holsters and radio receivers were patrolling the passageway leading to the offices and the booths. I waved my pass casually in the direction of the less daunting-looking of the two, but he directed me firmly but politely back to the accreditation desk, where I once again came eyeball to eyeball with the Asiatic-looking usher; pretending I'd made a mistake, I muttered an apology and went back towards the conference hall. I still had the headphones on, and Stauber's voice was ringing in my ears; he was talking about increased protection for sperm whales, of the strange habits of Boreal whales, of the impossibility of pinpointing the areas occupied by the white whale during the winter season, and of their mass destruction by the Inuit, who are gluttons for their skin, which they eat raw. But I could tell from the strained tone that his mind was on other things; he was shouting rather than talking, breaking off in mid-sentence and repeating the same word several times over. I imagined him up there in his booth, running his eye anxiously over the seats in the auditorium to see where I had got to; he had a lot of explaining to do. I paced up and down in front of the red curtain, uncertain how to proceed. I felt a sudden prickle of sweat break out all over my body, my mouth was dry and my tongue felt furry; seized with a spell of dizziness, I was forced to lean against the wall. I could feel one of my convulsions welling up in my chest; I tried to hold it back by breathing heavily, but already the first whistling sounds were escaping from my pursed mouth. My legs were trembling, my vision was becoming blurred; losing my step, I bumped into a group of people standing around the bar, one of whom helped me back on to my feet. I thanked them, shook myself free of their steadying hands, rushed to the cloakroom, collected my coat and ran out of the building, only to find myself pursued by the usher, demanding the headphones which I had forgotten to return. But while he was tugging me by the arm and calling the guards for help, I was already blurting out mangled, senseless words; grinding my teeth in an effort to contain myself, I fixed him with an angry, frightened glare, trying to shake off his hand. I pulled off the headphones and threw them towards him, running down the steps as I did so; at last he loosened his grip and bent down to pick them up. He watched me as I ran away, then went off again up the steps, shivering and turning up his collar, accompanied by the two nervous-looking guards who were already prattling into their radios.

I took refuge on a landing-stage from which I had a view of the esplanade in front of the conference centre; I sat down in the cold on a mooring-post, still breathing deeply in my attempt to ward off the attack. I had fallen over several times during my flight, tearing my trousers and grazing one of my hands on the gravel. I paused there for a moment, with the snow and the fine sand blowing into my eyes. Hugging my coat around me in an effort to keep warm, I kept an eye on the tinted windows beyond the black creek, and when I saw the first figures coming down the steps and on to the esplanade where a row of taxis was waiting for them, I stood up wearily, walked back towards a corner of the conference centre and positioned myself behind the hull of an upturned boat that had been pulled clear of the waterline; from where I stood I could distinguish the faces of the people who were emerging from the building. What I was seeking among the crowd who were shaking each other's hands and talking into their mobile phones, eyes on the middle distance, was Stauber's ruddy face, his short steps and awkward gait; but the esplanade was emptying out, and there was no sign of anyone who looked like him.

The last taxis were driving off, as were the last minibuses with the insignia of the various grand hotels; lights were going off in the foyer. I approached the building cautiously. Hugging the wall, I went back up the steps and slipped inside, pushing at the first door I came upon. I heard voices from inside the hall, some clattering and clanking, the echo of empty rooms. I hid between the pots of ornamental plants. A workman was pushing a trolley across the foyer, laden with assorted equipment; porters were shuttling to and fro, carrying piles of folders and files; behind his desk, the Asiatic-looking usher was putting the earphones back into their cases. Quaking with apprehension, I slipped past the screen previously manned by the two guards and went up the stairs to the interpreters' booths; clinging to the balustrade, dragging my aching leg, I proceeded to the corridor, lit now only by a few dim security lights. Above the window to each booth was a sheet of paper with the name of the language the interpreter had been translating from; I walked along the corridor until I came to the door of the German booth, noting that it was very slightly ajar.

I stopped, took a deep breath and listened hard, but all I could hear was the hum of a distant vacuum cleaner. In the auditorium behind me workmen were folding up the velvet curtains and loading them on to a trolley. I approached the door with extreme caution, doing my best to avoid making the boards creak. I leant against the wall and turned the handle, pushing against it with my shoulder, but it held firm; I peered in through the spy-hole, but could see nothing. I tried the door again with all my force, and this time it gave way; I stumbled in and fell upon something soft. In such faint light as penetrated through the tinted glass I recognised Stauber, lying on his back beside me; two fingers of one hand were caught in the lead of the microphone he still had twisted around his neck; his other hand was clutching the leg of a chair. Empty and rheumy, his half-closed eyes wore a surprised expression.

Floundering wildly, I edged away from the body, drew myself up to a sitting position and leant against the wall, panting heavily. The floor was scattered with papers, pencils and tattered dictionaries, clear evidence of a recent struggle. As I was struggling to get to my feet, I noticed a sheet of paper protruding from Stauber's jacket pocket; I pulled it out and held it up to the light. The list! The interpreter's list, yet again, but this time printed on art paper, with no crossings out.

Beside the city of Tallinn, an unsteady hand had added four strange names: Kim, Kaina, Leda and Ferdinand, this latter underlined. Scarcely had I recovered from this barrage of unexpected events than I heard the sound of steps in the corridor. Someone was coming, and they were coming fast; I glimpsed their shadow on the glass of the next-door booth. I heard the swish of fabric and the quick, laboured breathing of someone who has been running, then smelt the bitter smell of untreated wood mingling with the pungent scent of heated resin; it filled my nostrils, entered my brain, triggering off a rush of sights and memories.

It was him, the interpreter, right there, outside the door! He had killed Stauber and now he was coming to kill me! I thrust the sheet of paper into my pocket, jumped over the up-turned chair and pulled the door open, shifting the corpse as I did so in order to get out.

But the man I found before me was the Asiatic-looking usher, who jumped back in fright on seeing me and flattened himself against the wall. As soon as he recognised me, though, he seemed to recover himself, but when he saw Stauber's corpse he grabbed me by the lapels and let out a shriek. I tried to struggle clear, but the man had strong fingers, and all that I managed to do was to pull myself round with my back against the wall and push my aggressor towards the door of the booth. I could already hear the thump of the guards' boots on the stairs. I let myself fall heavily to the ground, taking the usher with me, then thrust him in the direction of the half-open door of the booth, where he encountered Stauber's lifeless arm. That caused him to loosen his grip; he crawled through the door into the booth, colliding with the chair, which then lodged itself in the door. I beat a hasty retreat, continuing down the corridor, to find, to my relief, that there was also a staircase at the other end; once down it, I hid myself among the ornamental plants which the workmen had assembled in front of the large windows, then rolled across the floor as quietly as I could until I found myself by one of the main doors. Looking up, I saw the two guards peering anxiously over the balustrade, seeking me out among the hopeless jumble of curtains, plants and crates scattered throughout the foyer. I waited until they had gone down the corridor to rescue the usher, then pushed open the main door and slipped out. There was one single taxi left on the esplanade; the driver had left the engine running to keep warm and was leafing through a newspaper, the air thick with smoke. I leapt aboard and shouted to him to drive as fast as he could to the timber wharf, n. 13.

The man with the rubber boots was talking Romanian; he looked at his watch and assured me that we would be in Warsaw by dawn. He was smoking and spitting into the snow, covering the traces carefully with his boots. The others nodded in agreement; their hands thrust deep in their pockets, they were prancing around in front of a bonfire which had been lit on the only remaining patch of concrete in a sea of ice-hardened mud. From behind mounds of earth, lorries were emerging, zigzagging over the steep terrain, their lights revealing a landscape of brushwood and scrap metal strewn around the remains of an old public weighbridge. It was Janos who had sent me to this god-forsaken place, promising that he would get me a passport and take mine in exchange; he had told me to ask for Radu, a Moldavian who helped illegal emigrants to cross the border and who would have me out of Ukraine within a few hours. A thickset, beefy man, he was greeted with universal deference when he jumped down from the first lorry without even waiting for it to stop, and a crowd gathered around him in a circle; he was wearing a fur cap with loose ear-flaps which hung to either side of his face like two deformed protrusions. The men then handed him bundles of banknotes which he counted rapidly before stuffing them in his pocket. Seeing me standing to one side, he gestured to me to come forward: 'Warsaw!' I said firmly; the circle opened up to let him pass. Radu positioned himself firmly before me, legs apart, and held out a bare hand with an expectant air.

'I have your name from Janos,' I said as quietly as I could, hoping the others wouldn't hear. Radu nodded and pulled me roughly to one side.

'It's five hundred for the journey, and a thousand for the documents,' he said quietly, looking me up and down with his small, bright eyes and counting out the banknotes suspiciously with elegant flicks of his fingertips. Then he produced a package from his pocket – it was wrapped in newspaper and bound with an elastic band – opened it and drew out a pristine new passport, which he handed me furtively. Shielding it with my coat, I peered at the green document which informed me, by the glancing light of the bonfire, that my name was now Tibor Preda and that I had been born at Galati on 30th November 1952. The photo on the first page was one that Janos had taken of me in front of the wall of a warehouse at the timber wharf. Radu was showing signs of impatience; he zipped up the inner pocket of his sheepskin coat and gabbled something I couldn't understand, pointing me in the direction of the third lorry, which was puttering away and emitting a considerable amount of smoke, its back wheels stuck in the mud. Keeping my eye on him, I went up to it, opened the door and climbed in; he stood there, still rubbing his hands, breathing on them for warmth; then at last he walked off towards the lorry in which he had come. I found myself sitting next to the man in the rubber boots, who was settling into his seat and wrapping himself up in a blanket.

'Now you can have a good sleep, and when you wake up we'll be in Warsaw, just in time for coffee!' he exclaimed, drumming his fingers on the face of his watch, then nudging the driver who was seated to his other side.

The man responded by drawing deeply on his cigarette; then, with a yawn accompanied by a sleepy chortle, he sunk his foot down on the accelerator; the engine gave out a loud clanging sound and the vehicle became wreathed in dense white smoke. Then the whole column moved off through a scattering of dismal empty blocks of flats, the lights of a goods yard revealing uncurtained windows and empty rooms littered with debris.

After a long detour around the city we took the trunk road going north; my travelling companion must have been used to such conditions, because despite the constant juddering and jolting, wrapped in his blanket he soon fell asleep. The driver chain-smoked but didn't utter a word; he drove with his forearms resting on the wheel; the cab was draughty, but the chill was lessened by a warm blast of stinking diesel coming from a fan below the dashboard. I too wrapped myself in a blanket I'd found on my seat, and huddled up against the door. It wasn't long before we were at the Moldavian frontier; it was five o'clock in the afternoon, but it seemed like the dead of night; the countryside was wreathed in a heavy layer of cloud. Through the mud-splattered window I glimpsed Radu at the barrier, chatting with a soldier wearing a large fur busby; they were laughing and gesticulating, giving one another hearty slaps on the back, their breath white in the light of the sentry box. The soldier leafed distractedly through the bundle of passports while the Romanian walked up and down in front of the barrier; then he nodded to the driver of the first lorry, who climbed down from his vehicle and went to deposit a crate in the boot of a car parked behind the customs shed. The soldier gave a salute and went back into his sentry box, and the barrier went up in front of the lorries.

We drove on through a dark plain, past the corrugated roofs of the occasional village which loomed up before our headlights like a vision and disappeared again instantly, swallowed up in the glare of the snow. In the light of a solitary street-lamp I glimpsed shadows walking along the edge of the road, pulling sledges laden with sacks; in the distance I made out the outline of a train, stationary and alone in the empty countryside.

After a long stretch during which I saw nothing but the tail-lights of the lorry in front of us, we reached the outskirts of a town; we crossed an iron bridge, on the other side of which I saw the outline of houses, shrouded in shadow. The road became narrower, running between buildings whose windows were plastered with advertisements, between crumbling walls and heaps of snow, past a large factory with lifeless chimneys; our headlights picked out packs of dogs which would scatter, barking, as we passed. When the houses began to thin out, we found ourselves in a large open space dotted with puddles and lit by the large neon signs of a petrol station; the lorries formed a slow-moving queue in front of the single pump, while the drivers banded into groups to smoke, hopping about in their efforts to keep warm.

We set off again along a road which soon became steep and, at times, winding; the vegetation became denser, and soon we found ourselves in a wood. We drove on for several more hours, and it's possible that I may have fallen asleep, between one jolt and another. I don't remember what time it was when the column drew up in a clearing in the middle of a wood; the headlights were turned off, and as soon as my eyes became accustomed to the darkness I could dimly make out the outlines of my companions as they climbed down from the lorries; my driver took his jacket from the hook, shook the man with the rubber boots and jumped down from the cab, leaving the door half-open. The air was intensely cold; a thick mist was swirling among the trees. Stiff and befuddled, I took a few steps to stretch my legs, then joined a small group of other travellers who were shuffling around in the snow, smoking and chatting in low voices. Some had gone off among the trees to urinate, others were producing their sparce rations and handing round a steaming thermos flask.

It was by pure chance that I noticed the black car parked on the other side of the road, its lights out but its engine still running; a slight plume of purple smoke was emerging from the exhaust pipe, and I could hear the slow beat of the pistons; inside, I could see the glowing tips of cigarettes. I was staring at it curiously when the man in rubber boots came up to offer me a mug of tea and a piece of bread imbued with just the faintest whiff of bacon; I thanked him and took an eager gulp of the hot sweet cinnamon-flavoured liquid. We stood beside each other, chewing in silence, under the pitch-black, ice-encrusted trees.

A sudden call rang out through the darkness and the lorries' engines were turned on again. Dim shapes came forwards through the snow and disappeared slowly behind the doors, which then banged shut. I too set off towards our lorry, following the man in the rubber boots, when I felt myself grabbed by the shoulders and forcibly dragged off; I tried to shout, to struggle free, but a sharp blow winded me.

The black car on the other side of the road started up its engine and skidded across the snow towards me; the door opened, and the man holding me by the shoulders thrust me into it; clutching me to him, he gave me a sharp punch in the stomach, stunning me and causing me to fall forwards, but firm hands slipped under my arms and pulled me on to the seat. I could feel someone rolling up my sleeve, could feel something cold slipping into a vein. I was dimly aware of the red tail-lights of the lorries as they drove off along the road; after that, nothing.

IV

It was the shooting pain in my wrist that woke me. I raised my head and saw my swollen hand shackled to the bedhead; using my feet for leverage, I managed to roll over on one side. I noticed that I was wearing nothing but a rough cotton gown that did up down the back; my legs were covered with an army blanket. The room was overheated, and a bitter smell of bleach mingled with musty plaster hung in the air; daylight was filtering in through frosted glass.

Twisting my wrist painfully in the handcuffs, at last I managed to sit up. Decrepit and filthy though it was, the place was clearly some sort of hospital. One corner of the room was strewn with shards of glass; there was a washbasin against one wall, and a little medicine cabinet on another with rows of small glass bottles. Piled up by a small fridge were several large plastic containers and a few packs of dry ice; a neon tube was flickering above a mirror near the door, sometimes almost fizzling out entirely, then springing back into life and sending out flashes of greenish glare. The middle of the room was occupied by an ancient, peeling operating table, with two tin buckets and a couple of rags positioned beneath the holes in its steel base; a circular lamp hung from the ceiling, which was covered in blackish mould following the outline of the beams.

The bed to which I was handcuffed was near the window; a fur coat hung from a hook in the wall. Somewhere outside, I could hear an engine turning over; then I heard steps approaching. I lay down again hurriedly and hid my face under the blanket; I could now hear voices, as well as steps. Then the door opened slowly, and a shadowy figure shouldered his way in, his hand on the doorhandle - a tall, bald man wearing a surgeon's gown, which he took off to put on the fur coat hanging from the hook.

He was talking quietly to someone I couldn't see. He crept up to the bed; I closed my eyes, pretending I was still unconscious. I could feel him taking my pulse, listening to my heartbeat. He bent over me and raised one of my eyelids, then drew back, addressing some remark to his companion, who interrupted him impatiently. They were talking Romanian, but I couldn't understand what they were saying. They argued briefly, then the other man seemed to give way. The door closed again; I heard steps going down the stairs, then the sound of an engine starting up and a car driving off. Then silence fell again, broken only by the clicking of the stove; yet I sensed that one of the two was still in the room.

Half-opening my eyes, I recognised Radu's fur cap; he was sitting on a stool and leafing through a bundle of banknotes, moistening his thumb with his tongue from time to time. He had taken off his jacket and hung it from the hook, on top of the surgeon's gown. He took his revolver out of his pocket and slipped it inside his cap, which he then placed on the floor. I moved very slightly, and he jumped. He raised his eyes to check that the handcuffs were still in place, then carried on with his counting; a phone buzzed in his pocket and he pulled out a large mobile, hiding his mouth behind his collar as he spoke.

'No, tomorrow. I've got to stay here tonight,' he whispered, but I caught his words.

'Nothing. We'll have to wait and see…' he added obliquely, holding the phone against his shoulder and wrapping the bundle of dollars in a handkerchief with his other hand.

'Yes, part of it. We'll get the rest tomorrow when the plane lands.'

He paused to listen for a time, puffing and panting, grinding away at the floor with his big boot.

'You'll just have to trust me! It's not my fault that it's foggy!' he said impatiently, picking up his cap and gun. Then he stood up sharply and left the room, banging the door behind him, but I just managed to catch his last remark:

'Listen, he can't operate until the plane arrives! Otherwise he says it'll fester, and the whole thing will be a write-off!'

It was then that I understood; I realised what they were talking about, and my blood froze in my veins. Radu had sold me to some organ-dealers; the man in the fur coat was to open me up and remove everything inside me that was saleable, liver, kidneys, eyeballs, the lot.

Then I realised what that room was fitted out for: I cast a terrified glance over the operating table, the tin buckets underneath the holes, the cabinet with the glass bottles, the jars of disinfectant, the dry ice and the plastic containers in which my organs would be sealed up. In one horrified flash, I imagined my body being laid out on that slab of steel and well and truly pillaged.

But after those first moments of panic, a feeling of resignation stole over me. The death towards which I was hurtling struck me as a gesture of mercy on the part of a distracted and powerless God: obliged to contract the damnation or redemption of his creatures out to inexpert angels, he must have noticed that, in my case, his deputies were going about it with a heavy hand, so he was doing his best to temper the misfortune from which he could no longer protect me. What he didn't seem to realise was that, in so doing, he was triggering another cataclysm, and in my heart I bitterly relished the idea that my infected organs would contaminate others with my vile disease: pieces of me would put down roots in alien bodies, and I would live on in their malady. I would proliferate, be fruitful and multiply, reducing one brain after another to mush, never to be snuffed out, never to be delivered from the verminous creepy-crawl of life. Through me, the bestial whistle would spread across the world like a wound; a hundred, a thousand whistling men would be born of my scattered tissues. It was I who was the source of the evil; I would branch out, lethally, tainting the defenceless fibres of humanity. I would send out my fearful whistles from a thousand mouths, I would see myself prosper from a thousand eyeballs, monstrous and base but ultimately untouchable. And how I wished I could be there when those looters of my body discovered what their fell deed was leading to; when Radu and the surgeon in the fur coat would have to account for their brutish error in front of their powerful clients!

The door was suddenly blown open by a draught, and a chill breeze filled the room; I shivered and pulled the blanket up with my free hand. Soon afterwards Radu returned, a rucksack on his shoulder; he glanced at me suspiciously, then picked up the stool and settled himself behind the bed, where he was out of view. I could hear him rummaging around, grumbling under his breath; after a while he came towards me with some biscuits, two wizened apples and a bowl of water. I ate and drank avidly; the last thing I could remember having in my stomach was the piece of bacon-flavoured bread given me by the man in rubber boots. I had no idea what time it was, nor how long I had been unconscious. Had I been abducted only yesterday, or had several days gone by since that dark afternoon in Odessa? I dozed off, and when I awoke it was beginning to get dark. My bones ached, my head was spinning and my throat was burning; I also felt distinctly sick. I wondered whether I was coming round from an anaesthetic: I was suddenly struck by the idea that the surgeon might have come back and started his butchering while I was asleep. Horrified at the thought, I clutched my stomach, turning a little as I did so, only to feel a sharp pain in my swollen wrist – I had forgotten about the handcuffs. I gasped with pain and curled up in the sheet, seeking relief on a cool corner of the mattress. Above all, they must not let me live – they could empty me of my organs, they could even take my blood, but they must not let me live thus maimed and blind. Terrified by these thoughts, I felt a roiling sensation in my stomach and began to retch.

'I'm sick!' I shouted, as a dark flood of liquid poured from my mouth, sullying the sheets and dripping on to the floor. I was aware of Radu jumping up behind me and shaking me viciously by the shoulder, swearing the while and looking around the room for something to clean up the mess. Heedless of the handcuffs, hoping to avoid further damage, he thrust my head over the edge of the bed, but it was too late, I was already soaked in vomit and a trickle of blood was running down my dangling arm. Losing all patience, Radu pulled the soiled sheet from under my stomach and threw it on the floor, kicking at it angrily with his boot; then he reached into his trouser pocket for the key, grabbed the handcuffs and unlocked them. Propping myself up on my elbows, I rubbed my aching wrist, but the sense of relief was short-lived: my jailer was now dragging me down from the bed and propelling me warily towards the door.

'Toilet, toilet,' he shrieked, cursing as he did so. We went out on to the landing, lit by a single fly-blown bulb; the lavatory was on the other side of the stairs. I noted that we were on the first floor of a crumbling prefabricated building which must once have been a clinic. The other rooms opening off the corridor no longer had any doors at all; a couple of rooms on the ground floor had their doors still hanging from them on rusty hinges. Inside them was assorted debris – broken glass, overturned metal cabinets and broken chairs.

The rain was pouring into the stairwell through a shattered skylight; above me I could see a patch of dull grey sky and, despite the biting cold, a barely perceptible stirring of fresh air gave me a feeling of relief. Here and there the aluminium banisters snaked downwards crazily, torn clear of their supports, or had tumbled down into the foyer below, to lie among scrap metal, plastic bags, lumps of masonry, empty tins and broken bottles; grass grew on the upper steps of a staircase which was brought up short by a tumbledown wall.

Barefoot, I picked my way cautiously through the debris-spattered mud with which the landing was strewn, with Radu tugging me impatiently by the hand; I wanted to beg him not to twist my arm, but as I opened my mouth to speak I sensed that I was about to be seized by one of my convulsions. I gave him a beseeching look, fearing that he might take it as some form of subterfuge and become violent, but I saw that he was even more frightened than I was, staring at me in terror and backing off. I held out my hands towards him; my tongue glued itself to my palate and my lips stiffened in a way that had become all too familiar.

I began to tremble uncontrollably; after a bit of confused gabbling, I produced the usual raucous braying which soon transmuted into a kind of whistle. My teeth were chattering so much that I spat out the remains of my food; I felt I was losing my balance, the world was swaying round me, the lavatory door, the landing, the dripping skylight. Seized by a fit of helpless coughing – now I could scarcely breath – and terrified of falling, I clutched at Radu's shoulders; to escape my grip, he started flailing around with his arms and knocked me sharply against the wall. As he retreated, he lent his back against the tottering banisters, lost his balance and toppled over the edge, pulling the wobbly banisters after him, while I carried on with my insane chirruping and gabbling, lurching around like one possessed.

When at last the spasms abated, I stood there in silence, listening to the sound of rain dripping on to sheet metal, to the rustle of plastic sheeting shifting in the wind. Aching in every limb, I made my way to the edge of the landing and peered cautiously over the edge, to see a black shape spread-eagled on its back amidst shards of broken glass, speared on the aluminium shafts, the rain gradually diluting the bright sticky stain which was spreading over the floor around him.

I teetered back into the room, closed the door and warmed myself up in front of the stove for a bit before cleaning myself up as best I could with the freezing water from the washbasin. Matters were not improved by the fact that I had cut both feet by walking on broken glass; I dabbed them with disinfectant and bound them up with gauze which I'd found in the cabinet. I picked up my clothes from the corner where they had been thrown – they were filthy, and damp, but I had nothing else I could put on. I picked up my empty wallet and Tibor Preda's passport and put them into Radu's rucksack; I also found the printed list I'd removed from Stauber's pocket; unsurprisingly, it was now somewhat the worse for wear. I took Radu's jacket down from the hook – it stank appallingly of sweat and dirt; rummaging around in the pockets, I found some car keys and the pistol, together with a bundle of banknotes, done up in a plastic band. I counted them out. Three thousand dollars – now I knew what I was worth, though the other half was yet to come. I took the handcuffs off the bedhead and put them too into the rucksack.

Suddenly the mobile rang, making me jump; I searched for it frantically in my inner pocket, then clutched it in my still trembling hand, watching it ring, feeling as though the unknown controller of my destiny were calling me from the other side, reproaching me, because that move had not been foreseen, and would be paid for dearly; warning me that, however I might struggle, however many Radus I might kill, I would not get away.

In those moments of confusion, dazed and relieved as I was by my unexpected escape, the one thing I felt clearly was a sense that I was no longer the person I had once been; at some moment to which I could not return, leaving my being unguarded, I had accidentally departed from it. Having moved on from my old self, I could now look upon it, empty, untenanted, an easy prey to others' whims. I felt that the ringing of the telephone had indeed been a warning, that soon I too would become a whistling man who would go to die in the convent in Odessa; on the one hand I had no way out, on the other I could afford the unheard-of luxury of playing with a life that was no longer my own. Spotting some bottles of aspirin on a shelf, I stuffed them into my pockets.

It was now dark outside. I put on the fur cap, took down a torch that was hanging on the back of the door and made my way cautiously downstairs. Keeping my distance, I shone the light in the direction of Radu's body where it lay in the dirt: he was still alive, one banister support protruding from his stomach. He was breathing unevenly, and blood was trickling from his mouth; his eyes were open, his expression almost resigned. Dazzled by the torchlight, he blinked; he seemed to be patiently waiting to die. Shivering with horror, I ran into the open, setting off an ominous clanging as I stumbled through scrap metal and tin cans, to find myself in a field furrowed with tyre marks. A thick mist was swirling over the grass, forming eerie configurations. Some distance away, I caught sight of the black car into which I had been unceremoniously bundled who knows how long ago. I got in and turned on the ignition; the lights lit up a gravel road. The engine sputtered for a bit, then the car sprang into motion with a throaty roar.

It was very dark. The road unrolled before me like a white ribbon in the mist; to either side, the headlights revealed frost-coated canebrakes. There didn't seem to be anyone else around. I was having trouble driving: my feet were hurting and my right leg quivered, unresponsive to my orders. Every so often it would stiffen on the accelerator, sending the car bounding forwards, then suddenly go limp, causing the engine to cut out. I had no idea where I was, I felt hungry and weak, but I drove through those frozen puddles hell for leather. The dashboard clock told me that it was ten o'clock, but that didn't help me with the day. It was almost midnight when I at last caught sight of a metalled road, not far away, beyond the canes; I wondered how long I'd been driving along beside it without noticing. Through the mist I glimpsed the yellow halo of headlights, then heard the welcome sound of traffic.

I turned off the headlights; leaving the engine running, I stretched out and fell asleep at last, though fear and exhaustion ensured that my sleep was not of the most restful, disturbed as it was by a series of hideous nightmares. When I woke up, dawn was beginning to break and the mist was thicker than ever; the branches of the trees were covered in hoarfrost, giving a certain beauty to the grim landscape. I got out of the car, climbed over the ditch and peered up and down the pockmarked road; there was a petrol station on the other side, with neon advertisements in a script I recognised as Cyrillic; there was also a rather dismal-looking bar. The neon flickered wildly, sending reflections skidding over the oily puddles. Two articulated lorries were parked some way away, liberally splattered with frozen mud; a little further off again were several rusty trailers perched on their stands. I hesitated: I didn't feel like driving, nor did I have the faintest idea where I was. I thought it might be better to try and hitch a ride, but I was nervous of coming out into the open.

I got back into the car, rummaged around between the seats and came upon a bottle of liqueur and some garlic sausage, both of which I attacked with considerable gusto. They warmed me and cheered me up; I was born aloft on an inexplicable wave of euphoria, raising the bottle to the windscreen to drink to that lackadaisical surge of good fortune which had insisted on saving me when the game was no longer worth the candle. I burst out into furious laughter, picking up Radu's pistol and aiming it into the void. Once again I heard the trilling of the mobile I still had in my pocket, and this time I managed to answer it.

'Radu is dead!' I shrieked into it in Romanian.

'Who's speaking?' asked a voice in tones of some alarm.

'Felix Bellamy! The man who killed Radu! The whistling man who will kill you all!' I shrieked again, guffawing as I did so.

Through the bar window I could see two men sitting on stools in front of the counter, wearing colourful tracksuits under loose windproof jackets; their bootlaces were undone, and they were staring blankly at the wall in front of them, sending the smoke from their cigarettes towards the ceiling. The bartender, a small bald man with a pockmarked face, was drying glasses and cutlery with a cloth; he stared at me absent-mindedly as I went in, adjusting his black waiter's waistcoat with a twitch of his shoulders. There was a welcome smell of smoke and coffee; reassured, I walked past racks of sweets and newspapers, to be informed by the clock on the wall that it was March 2nd.

As I sat down at one of the plastic tables by the window, pulling my chair out noisily, the other customers turned to look at me for a moment, then went back to drinking their coffee. They were talking German; probably the drivers of the two articulated lorries parked outside. I caught the barman's attention and pointed to the faded photograph of eggs and ham which was hanging above the coffee machine; he bent down behind the bar, I heard him opening a flap and soon afterwards he came to my table and banged down a plate which he'd just taken from a revolving oven. I devoured the half-cold eggs and half-burnt ham with relish, then sipped slowly at the watery coffee, warming my hands on the mug; in the meantime I was racking my brains for the best way to ask for directions without arousing suspicion. I looked around, seeking some point of reference, some clue as to where I might be. There were some dirty plates and a newspaper on the empty table next to me; I leafed through it, trying to decipher the Cyrillic letters – I would at least recognise the name Odessa, I imagined. I was looking at the pictures, at the diagrams with the weather forecast, when my own photograph leapt out at me from the middle of a page – the passport photo I had left with Janos. Under it, in a smaller format, was a photo of a card with Stauber's name badge on it, surrounded by indecipherable characters and big black headlines. I turned to look towards the bar; the two lorry drivers were still busy chatting, but the barman was looking at me. He was twirling the glasses around in the cloth and putting them back on the shelf, staring at me in the mirror as he did so.

I got up slowly, thinking that it would be better to pay and get out without further ado. I felt in my pocket for some money, and it was only then that I remembered that all I had was dollars; I peeled off a banknote without revealing the wad and put it on the counter, slipping my other hand mechanically into the other pocket and gripping the butt of the pistol.

The barman didn't bat an eyelid; he took the note with two fingers and expertly counted out the change, in *hryvne*, on the zinc. But as I leaned forwards to take the wad of dog-eared banknotes, I noticed another copy of the paper I had leafed through a moment earlier, propped up against the dishwasher beside the sink, open at the page with my all too prominent photograph. He intercepted my gaze and stiffened: he had recognised me. His lips began to quiver; rigid with fear, he stared at me as if he'd seen a ghost. At first I thought I might try to reassure him, so I lent up against the counter, seeking the right words; after all, I was the one who should be frightened.

But he was shaking his head and moving backwards, clutching at whatever came to hand. I pulled the pistol out of my pocket and pointed it in his direction, shouting as I did so. The man raised his hands and backed up against the shelf on which he'd been replacing the glasses. It was almost as though he wanted me to fire. He seemed calmer now, almost relieved. The lorry drivers had jumped down from their stools and come up to the counter, their hands above their heads. Uncertain of how to proceed, I waved the gun around and signalled to them to leave the bar, but they failed to get the message and scuttled around, white as sheets, shrieking the same word time after time; they took their wallets out of their trouser pockets and threw them down at my feet. Then finally they rushed outside, tripping clumsily over their bootlaces and knocking into tables as they did so. Shortly afterwards I heard their engines roar into life, then saw their lumbering vehicles bouncing over the potholes and driving out into the road, hooting loudly in the mist; they had left the door open behind them, and a blast of cold air blew in, causing the newspapers hanging from the rack to flutter wildly. My coffee was still steaming on the table; the barman was gazing at me imploringly.

Now somewhat at a loss, I pointed towards the till; the barman flicked open the drawer, then drew back and turned to face the wall. I went up to the till, grabbed a wad of banknotes at random and thrust them into my pocket; walking backwards, still with my gun trained on him, I picked up the lorry drivers' wallets and turned to run out of the door. I crossed the road, jumped over the ditch, leapt into the car and set off immediately along the canebrakes, still following the unmetalled road which ran alongside the main one, then branched out once more into the countryside.

For the moment, the mist showed no signs of lifting; the weak winter sun lightened it but never really broke through. By midday, though, the sky was dazzlingly bright, the light falling sharply on everything in sight and sending out cold reflections. An endless landscape of blurred fields sped past the windows; an occasional house loomed up through the purplish haze, then sank away into the blind eye of my rear-view mirror. I drove for hours without seeing a living soul, without encountering any other roads; sometimes a canal would appear to the side of the track, then wander off again to lose itself in meadows stiff with frost. Finally, in the distance, I saw a dense wall of tree trunks coming towards me through the mist, and found myself engulfed in a fir wood covering one slope of a hill, the road running up it in broad curves. When I emerged from the wood in a clearing at the top, I saw a broad plain stretched out below me, and a bend in a dark, muddy river flowing through fields lightly veiled by the tender green of the new corn. The track now ran downhill through leafless poplar groves, then joined a larger road covered with smooth, black asphalt. Just as I slipped into the flow of traffic, a pale sun finally revealed itself, causing the whole landscape to glitter unexpectedly: points of brightness sparkled on the recently upturned earth, on the metal of the cars, on the scrawls of ice in the ditches. At last I glimpsed a rusty signpost at the side of the road, and slowed down to read it: thirty kilometres to Suceava. Without noticing it, I had entered Romania.

After a dozen kilometres or so, I stopped to fill up with petrol and buy a few provisions. Going into the bar, I cast a nervous glance over its occupants, a tingle of excitement running down my spine. I fingered the gun in my pocket, feeling a nasty smile form on my lips; I ordered some sausage and coffee and ate hurriedly, glancing around warily as I did so. The barman had abandoned his post to go and wash the kitchen floor; I could see him through the half-open door. Such few customers as there were, were smoking in silence and drinking large tankards of beer. I put my cup on the counter and walked towards the door almost with regret, then turned to wink at the girl at the till, who picked up my crumpled banknotes hastily, pulling her cardigan over her chest in embarrassment. I drove out of the forecourt, past the garage building, parked behind an abandoned articulated lorry and locked myself in – it was time to get some sleep. I set off again around dusk, following the signs to the Hungarian border.

I still can't really understand how it was that I became a bandit. I was clearly drunk on the sheer thrill of risk taking. All sense of caution fell away, and I was gripped by an urge to risk my life in order to get the measure of the destiny that was dogging me. I enjoyed shuffling its cards, but in no way was I seeking a way out: rather than submit to the sentence it had in store for me, I preferred to cock a snook at it by laying myself open to an alternative, equally unpredictable downfall. Sated with the danger into which I was plunging so heedlessly, I forgot about the interpreter and Dr. Barnung; but I must admit that my criminal undertakings may also have been fed by a pinch of vanity. I even went as far as to think that, had my bosses back there in Geneva come to hear of them, they would have been proud of me. After all, they were forever urging me to try out new ideas. Inventiveness, daring, personal initiative, that's what all bureaucracies are lacking; I'd been hearing that for years. I was proud of this new skill I'd acquired entirely on my own; with a stab of annoyance, I even began to regret that I could no longer enter the lists for promotion to the post of director general. I committed every robbery hoping to read about it in the next day's papers, and at night I'd fall asleep imagining the headlines.

'Odessa murderer strikes again', 'Swiss criminal holds police at bay', 'Felix Bellamy, the Beast of Bucovina'.

I bought all the newspapers that mentioned me and piled them up on the back seat; I still have some cuttings, and carry them about with me in my wallet. I drove along highways and byways, pillaging shops, attacking stationary articulated lorries and isolated houses; but my true passion was the petrol stations on the A576. There was something particularly thrilling about training a gun on a roomful of people while the traffic rolled quietly by behind my back; someone might turn on me at any moment, one of the men I was threatening might pull out a gun himself, the police might burst in. In fact, none of this ever happened; those grim faces were afraid of me, people were quaking, some of them crying. They were at my mercy: I could kill them one by one with a bullet in the head or torture them slowly, firing at them limb by limb. I could do anything – except exchange my fate with theirs. I could have selected one of them at random, stuck my pistol in his hand and taken his place among the rest. I could have freed myself of myself, of that unknown me who was pursuing me, whose poisonous breath I felt upon my neck.

I always used the same strategy for my attacks: I'd hide the car in some track in the surrounding countryside and approach my goal by foot. I'd wait until there were few enough people in the service station for me to be able to observe them at length and assess their reactions. At such moments I felt strangely powerful: I was afraid of no one and nothing, not even of my convulsions, though these, it was true, were becoming increasingly few and far between. They added yet another grim note to the fear felt by my victims as, pistol cocked, I would begin to jabber and howl, wide-eyed and quivering. At such times, too, I felt my body monstrously enlarged; as though, until that point, it had been nothing more than a cold statue, and I had come into possession of it then and there. I saw my own flesh magnified as though under a microscope, my hairs like posts implanted in my skin, my wrinkles like canyons in a petrified desert, my bones like deformed encrustations created from a jet of red-hot lava which had suddenly solidified. When in the grip of such hallucinations I would note the tug of each muscle, the impulse of every nerve, taking stock of their efficiency, amazed by their effortless infallibility, surprised to find myself so resilient, my movements as deft and firm as those of a healthy man. A strange tingling sensation would creep along my limbs; they felt refreshed, as though cleansed of some lingering poison. It was as though all that was left of me was my body; something which had prevented it from developing was falling away. This hollow armature of flesh and bone was growing exponentially, capable now of unheard of feats.

Perhaps in fact one single shove would have knocked me off my feet; if one of my victims had had the courage to come up to me and twist my wrist I would have dropped the gun and fallen to my knees in pain, lain spread-eagled in the sawdust, alive yet dead, like a lizard's chopped-off tail. Sometimes a deathly chill would creep over me, as though I were turning to ice; but then the sheer thrill of the engagement would heat my blood, sending it beating through my temples, surging through my veins; I would stamp my feet wildly and shriek out my threats, clutching the butt of my gun and feeling that I too was made of gunmetal. I'd fire the odd shot in the confusion, picking off the glasses in their racks, or aiming at the electronic games. I didn't waste my bullets, though; I'd found some cartridge clips in Radu's car, but I was nervous about running out of ammunition. After my attacks I'd run away off into the countryside, lock myself in the car, hide the money and pistol under the seat and call a number chosen at random from the list on Radu's mobile:

'This is Felix Bellamy. I've just robbed the Astori Service Station on the A576. I'm the person who killed Radu, the one you wanted to chop up and sell by the kilo, the one who will eventually do for the lot of you, one by one!'

I'd burst out into peals of vicious laughter, turn off the phone, close my eyes and stretch out on the seat, waiting until the blare of sirens had died down on the main road. I'd set off again a few hours later, quite unfazed, driving coolly past the station I'd just ransacked. I often slept in the car; sometimes, when I felt insecure, I'd drive into a town, select a smart hotel and stay there for a day or two. I was sorry to have to throw Radu's mobile away when the battery ran down; it amused me to terrorise his friends with my phone calls. But by now I no longer needed to build up a reputation; at least some of the fur-hatted surgeon's henchmen would not have had a good night's sleep for quite some time.

For the brief period when I was travelling the roads of Romania like a buccaneer, my physical problem seemed to vanish. My convulsions became rarer, I no longer suffered from nausea or dizziness; even the raging sweating fits to which I had previously been subject, leaving me in a state of utter prostration, suddenly stopped. I had a hearty appetite, and fell into a deep and dreamless sleep the moment my head touched the pillow. I would wake up refreshed, clear-headed, my mind crystalline as the morning air. I'd get back into the car and set off on my looting sprees as though they were my daily task, a new profession I had found for myself, one which I practised scrupulously and well. It was as though I were in the grip of a sort of hypnosis, as though I were obeying an instinct. I knew that what I was doing was monstrous, but I had no sense of guilt; taking out my gun and pointing it at the defenceless clients of the petrol stations I found along my way had become a bodily need, an impulse I could not resist. I was acting like an animal; for the few minutes my assaults lasted, I truly felt that I had been transformed into some lesser being. I must have cut a terrifying figure, because people backed off even before I pulled out my gun. Perhaps my face took on the rapacious look of the interpreter, perhaps, like his, my words came out as eldritch howls; yet when I looked at myself in the rear-view mirror when I got back into the car, my face looked completely normal, and it was only slowly that I realised what I had done. My baffled mind was a brazier in which a great fire had at last been extinguished, still clouded by dense smoke; all that remained after such devastation was shrouded in fog.

I was going to have to get rid of Radu's car; it was beginning to arouse suspicion, even in the remote mountain service stations where I went to fill up with petrol to avoid the A 576. One afternoon, driving towards Cluj where I was intending to spend the night, I noticed the hangar of a brand new shoe factory just off the road, with several luxury cars with foreign number plates parked outside. I turned off the engine and peered at the prefabricated building through the wire netting. Suddenly I heard a blind go down, then, one by one, all the lights went out. I picked up Radu's rucksack, got out of the car and slithered down the grass bank until I came to the point where the wire netting ended.

I saw a group of people come out of the building and gather for a few minutes on the gravel, chatting and smoking before throwing down their butt ends and getting into their cars, driving off rapidly down the road which was now vanishing into the evening mist. Once clear of the gates, one of them – a grey Mercedes – had drawn up in the darkness to the side of the little road, well clear of the streetlights. A man got out, holding a mobile phone to his ear, walking and talking at the same time, staring at the tips of his shoes.

I ran down the hill a little further and took up a position at the edge of the ditch, in order to have a better view. I couldn't see anything inside the car; the tinted windows reflected dark reddish clouds. The man carried on talking. Numb with cold as he probably was, he had one of his hands in his pocket. I could see his breath above the boot; I leapt across the ditch, threw open the car door and jumped in, hearing him shout as I turned the engine on. I heard gunfire, and a bang on the boot lid; while I was watching the man turn around and try vainly to run after me, I felt a pair of cold hands pressing on my throat, and pointed nails digging into my eyes. I braked sharply, turned round on the seat as best I could and directed a few vicious punches in the direction of my assailant before driving on at speed, my tyres smoldering on the asphalt. I hit something soft and yielding, whose scent would linger on my sleeve for quite some time. I heard a gasp, a coughing fit, and then a feeble moan from time to time. I left the A576, drove up into the mountains for a few kilometres and stopped at the edge of a village; I got out of the car and opened the back door, to find a young girl curled up on the seat, just visible in the yellow glow of the safety light. I made a cautious move in her direction, but she instantly began kicking and shrieking like a madwoman.

Afraid of attracting attention, I got in and drove off again, in search of a suitable place both to rob a Romanian car and to rid myself of my unwelcome visitor. I drove slowly, down dark empty roads, through nameless villages, past isolated farms, by empty haylofts and old agricultural machinery sunk in the dripping mist of dismal fields.

'I didn't mean to hurt you!' I tried saying in Romanian, peering at my prisoner in the rear-view mirror, but she was too terrified to answer; she was breathing with difficulty and sobbing quietly.

'Don't be afraid. I won't come anywhere near you!' I insisted. 'All I'm interested in is the car. As soon as we're back on the main road I'll let you out, I promise!'

That seemed to calm her down, though she continued sobbing; she sat stock-still, watching my every movement.

'And where would you drop me? On the roadside?' she asked after a bit.

'I'll drive you wherever you want to go,' I told her gallantly.

'I want to go to Cluj, to my hotel,' she said testily, between sobs.

'I can't go to Cluj with this car, at least not until I've changed the number plate. I'd have the police straight on my tail!' I objected politely but firmly.

'So what are we going to do?' she asked plaintively.

'Haven't you got a mobile?' I was beginning to lose patience.

'The battery's flat. And my clients are waiting for me at Cluj, for a working dinner!' Now she too was becoming angry.

'Then I'll take you back to the factory and you can phone from there for someone to pick you up,' I suggested.

'The factory will be closed by now!'

'There must be a guard. We could break a window!' I snapped back, irritated by her quibbles.

Drying her eyes, she nodded. I heard her blowing her nose; her breathing was now almost normal.

I turned the car round in search of a road that ran downhill. It was raining heavily; the headlights served almost no purpose, staining the mist yellow but not shining through it.

'We can talk French if you prefer,' the girl said suddenly, in perfect French.

I raised my eyes to look in the rear mirror, seeking her out in the dark.

'French? Are you French?' I asked more cordially, delighted to have a chance to speak my native tongue.

'No, I'm Romanian. I'm an interpreter.'

At those words, pain blossomed in my stomach, a short-lived cramp clenching my vital organs.

'An interpreter?' I repeated blankly.

'What about you? I don't think you're Romanian. Am I right?'

'No, I'm not Romanian,' I answered absently, and left it at that.

No sooner were we down in the valley than I noticed I had a flat tyre. I found a spare one in the boot, but I didn't feel confident that the car would perform well if it came to a chase. The situation was touch-and-go; to add to my worries, there was that unintentional hostage. Swearing to myself, I changed the wheel, realising now that instead of going back to the factory I would do better to get myself another car. The girl was watchful, glancing nervously out of the window. Down here on the plain too it was raining heavily, obliging me to reduce my speed. Peering into the darkness, I tried to work out where we were. Beyond a curve in the road I saw the illuminated sign of a decrepit service station, and slowed down; through the streaming windows I could just make out the figure of a mechanic, seated in front of a television. Two cars were parked under the canopy. I veered off the road and swerved into the muddy forecourt, turned off the engine and twisted round in my seat, switching on the safety light. It was then that I had my first good view of her: she had large, troubled eyes, light skin and an unruly black fringe. Her features were delicate, but she had a cold expression on her face. Something about her made me feel uneasy, as though it were she who had the upper hand. Unable to hold her gaze, I pretended to be scanning the darkness beyond the window.

'Look, why don't you go and call your friends? Then you can come back and wait for them here in the car.' She looked at me suspiciously and seemed about to get out, but then hesitated.

'What about you?' she asked, although she didn't look at me.

'Don't worry about me. I'll be off – and I'm sorry about the mix-up,' I said, holding my hand out stupidly towards her above the seat.

She stared at me thoughtfully, biting her lip, looking now at me, now at the lights in the bar. Clutching her handbag to her, she thrust a shoulder to the door and clambered out; I watched her bedraggled figure disappear into the darkness, then got out myself and went up to the two cars. I hadn't noticed it from the road, but the larger one was raised up on a jack. The other was an old Alfa Romeo; the door was unlocked and I climbed in and sat down in the dry. I wanted to wait for the girl to come back and get into the safety of the car before going to force the mechanic to give me the keys. But there was no sign of her, and I was beginning to lose patience. The rain was hammering down loudly on the metal roofing; beyond the wall of water I could just make out the glass door to the service station.

Suddenly, amidst the din of the water crashing from the eaves, I heard a cry. I leapt out of the car and stumbled through the mud, flinging myself into the service station, pistol cocked. The girl was stretched out on the damp sawdust in a state of semi-undress, with the mechanic on top of her, holding her by the wrists. Seeing me, he tried to get to his feet, but got caught up in his trousers and fell back on his knees; his forearms on the ground, he gave me a doltish stare. Without thinking what I was doing, I began to kick him in the face, but instead of defending himself he just lay there motionless, as though impervious to my blows, and that made me more furious than ever. Had the girl not shaken me from my trance-like state with a loud cry, I would have kicked the man to death. As it was, though, I turned my attentions elsewhere, leaving him groping about on the floor, his face covered in blood; I rushed over to the counter and rummaged through the drawers until I came upon the bunch of keys with the Alfa Romeo shield. While I was about it, I thought I might as well make off with the takings into the bargain, together with a wallet lying on a nearby chair. Then I rushed out, dragging the girl behind me, switched on the engine of the Alfa, parked beneath the dripping awning, and set off hell for leather towards Cluj.

My prisoner was now crying harder than ever, pulling her sopping jacket across her chest.

'My handbag! I've lost my handbag!' she wailed, running her hands desperately over the seats.

Driving was becoming all but impossible; the road was a mass of huge puddles. My wheels sank into the mud and disengaged themselves with loud sucking noises, sending me skidding across the road. I no longer had the faintest idea of where I was, and would drive pointlessly towards any light I saw looming through the wall of water. I'd been driving for almost an hour when I realised that I'd overshot Cluj by quite some distance: we were now on the minor road to Oradea.

The radio was announcing accidents and traffic jams, caused by the monumental downpour that had unleashed itself on the region. The seven o'clock news bulletin also made mention of my latest exploit.

'The Beast of Bukovina has struck again, this time with the help of a mysterious accomplice. The police found documents and personal effects belonging to a Romanian citizen, a certain Magda Kobori, on the scene of the crime. According to evidence given by the victim, Bellamy is using the woman as a decoy,' said the announcer.

'This is too dreadful! What sort of a pickle have you got me into now? You're a raving lunatic! Why on God's earth did you attack that man? And now I'm your accomplice! Me, a gangster's moll...' Then her tone changed, becoming almost a murmur:

'I... I wanted to thank you...' She gave a lengthy sigh and dissolved into tears again, but this time more gently, in a way that I found touching: a survivor's tears of sheer relief.

'So you're the Beast of Bukovina!' she exclaimed incredulously, reverting a little to her former self.

'Pleased to meet you, young lady! My name is Felix Bellamy. Believe it or not, I'm a peace-loving Swiss citizen who, until recently, practised one of the most trouble-free professions in the world!'

Oradea was awash with swirling water. The river had broken

its banks further upstream, sweeping away the electricity pylons. As we approached the centre we noticed a hotel with its lights on, but felt nervous about going in. I told Magda to get out, then drove on for a few metres and left the Alfa in a supermarket car park. I went back to the hotel and asked for a single room, pretending not to recognise the pretty girl who was registering at the reception desk, complaining about the loss of her luggage in the chaos. A few moments later, she came to knock on my door.

'It's impossible to make a call; the line is down and won't be mended until tomorrow!' she told me in a state of some alarm. I don't know how I found the courage to pull her into the room; her expression was cold and resentful, as though she expected it. I removed my hand from her arm and took a few steps back.

'I imagine I owe you something,' she said in a quiet but steely voice.

I felt ridiculous; I lowered my eyes, desperately thinking of something to say.

But it was she who came towards me; I caught her smiling a shop-girl's smile, perfidious yet beckoning. Caressing my sides, she pushed me on to the bed and turned out the light. She dealt with my body's needs briskly and deftly, while revealing none of her own. Then she pulled the mattress on to the ground and went to sleep on the other side of the room, as far away from me as she could.

Each evening of our stormy enforced joint adventure, Magda extracted my pleasure from me almost by force, without waiting for me to ask it of her; she fought off my amorous approaches speedily but effectively in the pitch darkness, with me clinging pointlessly to a body which seemed insensible to my touch. I ran my hands over her as though by so doing I would be able to remember it for ever. Rancour at her indifference goaded me to resist, to put a curb on my own senses; but I always yielded to her business-like expertise. A cloud of unworthy thoughts would float through my mind, and I would make a show of driving them away, only to let them resurface when I was back at the wheel, driving along the flooded roads of the Banat. At times I would be bedevilled by a chilling desire to do her harm, to finish the grim work begun by the mechanic on the sawdust-strewn floor of the service station; on other occasions I would dream obscurely of forging myself an existence by her side. In my unbridled daydreaming I would imagine myself with a grey office in a white corridor in the shoe-factory building; Magda and I would live in a house exactly like my own, with roses, and a lake; or perhaps in Constanta, by the sea Roxana had described to me and which I'd never seen. But here my daydreaming would be brought to an abrupt stop by the idea of living with an interpreter: I was haunted by the irrational fear that anyone dedicated to that unhealthy profession could bring me nothing but harm. After all, if I was running amok with every police force in the Carpathians on my heels, whose fault was it but that of an interpreter?

At first light I peered through the shutters to see a dismal expanse of mud: grey houses and office blocks reflected in motionless water. Magda was asleep; my head still full of dreams, in the half-light I thought that the body lying beside me under the covers was that of Irene. My thoughts wandered skywards, lifting me far above that drab hotel, above the town and further still, into an aeroplane, so that the desolate roads I had been driving along were now no more than brownish scribbles in a sea of mossy green. Then, in a flash of clarity amidst the inchoate clouds that were my thoughts, for a moment I saw myself, alone in a strange land, playing the bandit. I looked incredulously at my disaffected body, apparently now cured; I opened my hands and became absorbed in the network of lines I saw there. Were they still my own? I listened nervously to my heartbeat, thinking I detected a new violence in it. Perhaps this recklessness was simply the new form my illness had assumed. In order to escape me, rather than transforming my body, it had transformed itself. Coming up against the dogged resistance of a disordered will, it had tried to attack me in a more cunning fashion; now it was altering my perception of things, seeping into my mind, first squeezing out the less essential substances, those fostering common sense and moderation, then moving on to the juices of consciousness and memory. If, for the moment, I was a mere bandit, perhaps I would soon become an out-and-out assassin, a sadistic torturer.

It was Magda who aroused me from these thoughts; she had woken up suddenly, and wanted to go down to the reception desk to try the phone again. We dressed in haste, in silence, almost without looking at one another. We crouched down behind the half-open door, then went out into the corridor one after the other. I went down first, but on the stairs I heard the porter repeating the number of Magda's room, and her name, in tones of some alarm. I sat down on a step and peered into the foyer: two policemen were positioned by the entrance, while another four were preparing to come up the stairs, taking their pistols out of their holsters as they did so; another was keeping an eye on the lift. A police officer in a black raincoat was glowering at the photo in the newspaper the porter had opened up before him. I beat a hasty retreat in order to warn Magda, then, turning round, noticed a little flight of metal stairs by the lift-shaft, leading to the basement. We crept down the metal stairs; above us we could hear hurried steps, doors banging, policemen shouting. We scrambled through a window, ran through the mud to the supermarket car park and drove off into the blue yonder, amidst a blare of sirens from fire engines and ambulances which were foundering in the puddles and sending murky ripples eddying around them.

I was driving through a dim blur of flooded fields, the wrecks of floating cars and uprooted pylons, trying to get my bearings, when I heard Magda burst into sudden laughter behind me in the back. I glanced into the rear-view mirror: I thought I caught a glint of ferocity in her eyes, a flash of cruelty.

'Felix Bellamy, now that I'm the accomplice of the Beast of Bukovina, I want to carry out a robbery of my own! I want to see people falling to their knees in front of me, I want to shoot at windows and glasses and mirrors! I want to smell the scent of fear, of blood, of gunpowder! Stop – I want to come in front!' I heard her shout.

As the road curved steeply down a long hill, we saw a service station on the outskirts of Salinta; Magda went in first to ask for directions. Several foreign lorry-drivers were camping out in the place, immobilised by the bad weather; their vehicles were parked in the space behind the petrol pumps, wheels sunk in the mud. I burst in a few seconds after her, pointing my pistol at their dull-eyed, weary faces.

'Throw your wallets on to the floor and you won't come to any harm!' I shouted. Magda turned away from the counter and walked around among the tables, translating my threat to our astonished crowd of victims in several languages. I heard her speaking German, English, Italian and Dutch, and realised that she must have looked at the number plates of the lorries before coming in.

That evening, in a hotel in Arad, we read the headlines in

the *Jurnalul National*: 'Country cut in two by floods – traffic at a standstill'. Then, lower down: 'Bonnie and Clyde of the Carpathians still up to their monkey business with the police – Swiss bandit and accomplice sighted at Oradea – petrol station plundered'. I read the entire article and discovered to my fury that I was being held responsible for Radu's death as well: 'Ravaged body of lorry driver from Chisinau murdered by Swiss thug found in Ukrainian countryside', was how the journalist put it. Below was a passage in italics which I have in my wallet to this day:

In these difficult times, our hapless country has suffered all manner of woes, from corruption to economic decline, from unbridled pollution to the most savage violence. Having rid ourselves of dictatorship, we deluded ourselves that the worst was over, and that a new prosperity might dawn at last, even in this dismal land. But, given half a chance, the first thing our people do is emigrate, which is their only chance of giving their children a decent future; our orphans are dependent upon charity. We have become a repository of cheap labour for the rich countries, in a word, we export poverty – that is our greatest resource. Everything else must be imported. Except for criminals, that is: our home-grown type is every bit as competent as the imported variety, and certainly more respectful of local customs. Above all, they go about their business in a more mannerly, more elegant fashion, homing in on ministries rather than on highways; using paper rather than guns. Lulled into a sense of false security, the Romanian people still feel that there is some point in going to work; basically, this too is a form of ethical behaviour, and in the long term – all forms of social evolution are slow-moving – some good is bound to come of it. We knew that the Swiss

*made chocolate and founded the Red Cross; that they were
partial to orderly traffic and neat flowerbeds. Now we know
that even the snow-clad Alps may breed outlaws of the most
murderous stripe. The base individual who is terrorising our
roads offends us more by his provenance than by his turpitude;
his forays wound our national pride more than they do our
pockets, because even the poorest Swiss lives like a nabob
in comparison to his Romanian equivalent, and if there was
one humiliation we had yet to experience, it was that of being
robbed by a descendant of William Tell. How many Romanians
will Felix Bellamy still have to rob before he amasses the
booty he would acquire by robbing one single man in his
own country? Why carry on targeting the ill-stocked coffers
of failing petrol stations or the grubby wallets of a few lorry
drivers when he has friendly dealings with banks and ciphered
accounts? Clearly, we've entered the age of globalisation with
a vengeance, we are part of a game which is no longer under
our control. Thus we find ourselves almost regretting our
own well-upholstered ministerial thieves; they were almost
appealing in their restraint. But looking at it from a strictly
economic point of view, what interest would a Swiss thief have
in coming here? Of course it must be easier to gull our poor
ill-armed police, to dupe our down-and-out secret services,
to shake off our ramshackle black Marias with sleek foreign
vehicles than it would be to challenge the well-trained, well-
equipped Swiss federal equivalent. Felix Bellamy, if you're a
man, take yourself off to Norway or Liechtenstein, and leave
us to starve in peace.*

We were now hell-bent on thievery; Magda took an insane
pleasure in it, as indeed did I. After each strike, she'd leap
into the car holding her breath in her trepidation, fear and

excitement written on her every feature; then, as soon as we were at a safe distance, she would burst into laughter, banging her fists on the seats in jubilation and shouting out curses. She had persuaded me to let her hold the gun, and I felt she cut a stylish figure when she planted herself at the counter, legs apart, gripping the weapon with both hands. I trusted her; I sensed that she had an innate love of danger, but that she also knew how to change course rapidly if circumstances required it. I didn't even resent the fact that she would waste cartridges by shooting at windows and electronic games. She was capable of carrying out robberies entirely on her own, and I let her have her head; all I could do was follow her – it was she who was now the ringleader.

One afternoon we stopped in a small town near the Hungarian frontier, eating hamburgers in the car. The weather was strangely mild; on the rust-coloured hills, at the edges of muddy fields the odd bush was becoming white with blossom. A misty plain stretched out to either side of the road, an unforgiving landscape touched with spring. I opened the car door and breathed in the pungent smell of a canal.

'The train to Cluj stops not far from here. Your things will still be in the hotel. You can tell the police the whole story; your clients from the Bistrita factory can testify that I held you prisoner,' I suggested, turning to look at her. A light wind lifted her hair.

'Is that what you want, for me to go?' she asked, her mouth full of hamburger.

'That's the only way you can save yourself,' I said quietly, looking away. Still chewing, she gave me a suspicious stare, then screwed up the greasy paper and threw it out of the window.

'Save myself? What from?'

'From a future you don't deserve. From me, from the death sentence I'm dragging behind me!'

'No one will save me from this hour of the afternoon, when the light hurts your eyes and it's too early to sleep, but too late to get out of bed. The towns are empty, the houses are sad and quiet, all you can hear is ticking clocks. Have you ever made love at this time of day? It's a disaster.' At these last words, a cold note crept into her voice.

'They won't keep you in prison for long.'

'It's not prison I'm afraid of. I was born in prison. How can I describe the utter bleakness of a courtyard cut in two by a washing-line, of gravel which screeches when you trample it, of the nuns giving me reproachful looks because I'm making the gravel cry, and I'm crying myself, which is tantamount to insulting their generosity?'

A fixed, blank look had come into her eyes; she was savouring those words as though they'd been a long time in the making.

'You could go back to your job,' I insisted stubbornly, trying to distract her from her gloom.

'Job? What job?' she asked mockingly.

'I thought you said you were an interpreter? Weren't those people in the factory your clients?' I asked in bewilderment.

She bent her head and glanced at me out of the corner of her eye, resting an elbow on the top of the open window.

'Ah yes, an interpreter… or a whore. It depends on the day. But everyone's a client! And I can enchant the lot of them in this or that language, because I speak them all!' She burst into dirty, vulgar laughter; the more she laughed, the more her laughter sounded like crying in disguise. I turned on the engine to cover the sound and drove on as fast as I could

among the slow-moving lorries, which flashed their lights at me in annoyance as I wove between them.

It all came to a tragic end one morning at dawn in Timisoara. For reasons of security we had decided to sleep separately, in neighbouring motels just outside town, not leaving our respective rooms during the night. We wanted to try to get into Yugoslavia, but we needed another car; we'd been travelling in the same one for two days now. We'd driven into the outskirts of town; I'd got out of the car at the corner of a low building and positioned myself in a doorway, prior to forcing the first wretch who came out to hand over the keys to his car. Magda was waiting for me on the other side of the road with the engine ticking over, ready for a getaway if anything went wrong. We were surrounded by a sea of blocks of flats where lights were gradually going on, revealing bare kitchens, unmade beds, women in dressing-gowns. A factory siren hooted in the distance; a train was rattling by to the other side of a bedraggled field.

Then I saw a light come on in the hallway, and flattened myself against the wall. But just at that moment two fast-moving cars appeared at the end of the road, driving without headlights; I heard the roar of their engines before I actually saw them. Magda noticed them too late; she was trying to drive over to me, tyres screeching, but she got wedged under the protruding trailer of an oncoming articulated lorry.

The two cars placed themselves crosswise, trapping her completely, and blue lights started flashing; another police car appeared almost silently from a side-street. It drove up on to the pavement, scraping its underside as it did so, then on to the patch of grass behind the building, becoming all but lost in the tall weeds.

It could only be me they were looking for. On the road, car doors were banging shut one after another. People were shouting; chrome weapons were glinting in the cold dawn light. Four or five policemen were positioned to the sides of the cars, peering cautiously in the direction of their prey. People were now coming out of the blocks of flats, gathering in curious groups on the pavement. I had hidden under a parked car, but now I slithered out and joined the group of onlookers who were gathering around the cars. In the ensuing chaos, although I was trying to keep clear of the fray I found myself being jostled to the front.

The policemen were now right in front of me, and it was at that moment that I caught sight of Magda coming into the middle of the road. She was holding her hands above her head and walking in the direction of the cocked pistols. The policemen were conferring by means of shouted messages; as soon as they were sure she was not armed, two of them fell upon her, thrusting her arms behind her back, putting them in handcuffs and shoving her in the direction of one of the police cars. It was then that we saw each other, my face just a foot away from hers. Dazzled by the headlights, the crowd pushed forwards for a better view, while the police tried to disperse them, fending them off with truncheons. Nobody noticed the glances Magda and I exchanged. I shall never forget that last smile she gave me – it even had a touch of sweetness to it, as though she wanted to express her thanks. What for, I do not know. Who knows who or what Magda really was, and what became of her.

Profiting from the confusion, I pushed back through the crowd and slipped between the cars in the car park until I was at the back of the block of flats; the police car, I noted, was now driving away. When the crowd began to disperse I walked across the grass and down the escarpment, climbed over the fencing and on to an open wagon which was moving slowly along the tracks in front of the goods yard. Stretched out on the rough planks jolting noisily beneath me, I stared at the yellow horizon; plunging backwards through time, I was reminded of that freezing morning in Odessa. As though the days of my Romanian forays had never existed, I suddenly realised that I must get back to Dr. Barnung's clinic – as soon as possible.

I arrived in Belgrade one Sunday afternoon. I looked for a hotel and bought a rail ticket for Munich the very next morning. Before getting on the train I also purchased a suitcase, some clothes and a spongebag. At the station I just had time to dash into a barber's, and when I looked at myself in the mirror in my wagon-lit I thought I looked the perfect commercial traveller. At the Austrian frontier Tibor Preda's passport aroused the suspicions of a diligent customs officer, who examined it at length and radioed his superiors; but Radu's friends must have been true professionals, because he could finally find no fault with the little green document for which I'd paid five hundred dollars. After inspecting my luggage with minute care, he could do nothing except wish me goodnight, close the door to my compartment and climb down from the train.

The nurse at the reception desk told me that Dr. Barnung was away at a conference and would not be back until the end of the month. I glanced through the glass partition into the corridors – same old lino, same old light wooden furnishings. Yet everything seemed strangely different. I asked to speak to Frau Goldstein.

'One moment, please,' said the nurse, picking up a phone. The red-haired woman who came towards me in the porter's lodge was a complete stranger to me.

'Are you Frau Goldstein?' I asked in amazement.

'What is it you want?' she asked curtly.

'I'd like to see Mr. Ortega,' I said, equally brusque.

'There's no Mr. Ortega here,' she shot back, shaking her head.

'All right then, Mrs. Popescu. Is Roxana Popescu still in the German section?'

'I'm sorry, sir, I don't know what you're talking about; and anyway, we're not allowed to issue information concerning our patients,' she snapped virtually pushing me out of the lodge.

She closed the glass door and went off down the corridor towards the lift. Undeterred, I went out into the road and round to the back of the building, where Dr. Barnung had his consulting room. The blinds were down; the letterbox was stuffed with mail of every kind. I rang the bell repeatedly, then peered into the waiting-room for signs of life. Nothing. In the half-light, everything seemed to be just as it was at the time of my first visit; even the magazines on the table seemed to be the same. I walked off in utter bewilderment, and wandering round the tree-lined avenues and trim little villas I finally realised that I was lost; I had to walk a long way before I found a bus stop. When it was dark, though, I went back to the villa, with a jemmy and a torch I'd bought in a hardware shop. I climbed over the garden fence and went round to the back of the building. I recognised the window to Dr. Barnung's study, the windowsill where the cat had been dozing on that long-ago winter afternoon when Dr. Barnung had given me his diagnosis. I forced the blind and climbed into the consulting room, to find the same old heavy wooden furniture, the same prints of the birds of prey. I was looking for the filing cabinet, which I remembered as being near the window. I leafed through the files and found the letter 'B', but there was no folder with my name, nor was there anything on Ortega, Vidmajer, Vandekerkhove or Popescu. There were plenty of unknown names, though, and the dates when their owners had been admitted were all subsequent to my departure, as though the original patients had been replaced by others within a matter of weeks. I closed the filing cabinet and slipped out, squeezing myself under the blind.

No sooner was I back on the road than I heard a rustling sound behind me. I jumped aside and ducked, then rolled along the grass, trembling with fear, only to catch a brief glimpse of a figure crouching behind the hedge. I ran off at breakneck speed, but soon I could hear footsteps other than my own, and my pursuer's laboured breathing; to my horror, he was gaining ground. I hurtled down the empty road as fast as my legs would carry me, among parked cars and dark gardens, trying to put more space between me and the man behind me and reach the lit avenue I could see beyond the trees. But at a turn in the road I found myself confronted by two other shadowy figures blocking my path.

Someone punched me in the stomach, winding me; I fell to the ground amidst a hail of blows from boots that were all too solid, tried vainly to extricate myself from the clutch of hands which were dragging me along the asphalt; desperate by now, I covered my head with my arms and sank down against a car in some attempt at self-protection, only to find that someone was going through my pockets and virtually pulling the clothes off my back. I heard an exchange of muffled remarks, a bit more panting and gasping, a shuffle of confused footsteps and then the men moved off into the darkness.

I ran my hands cautiously over my aching body; blood was

running into my eyes, blurring my vision. Pulling myself up by a nearby railing, I managed to get to my feet; but not for long. I'd only gone a few dozen yards before I was obliged to stretch out on the damp grass of a strip of greenery at the edge of the road. With difficulty, my hands found their way into my pockets – all the money had gone, even the notes I'd put into an envelope and attached to the inside of my belt. I looked up at the star-filled sky, wondering how my own star could possibly have sunk so low.

I could at least go back to my hotel and retrieve the odd garment and Tibor Preda's precious passport. I sold such items as I could and left the rest, slipping out of the hotel by night without paying the bill and spending time begging at the station, where I soon made friends: two of the porters, the woman at the paper stall, the Turk who cleaned the lavatories. Thanks in part to them, I managed to scrape together enough to live on; but the problem was where to sleep, because I couldn't stay in the station overnight, and had to wander into dangerous outlying areas to take shelter in old factories or under viaducts.

I went back to the clinic on numerous occasions in search of Dr. Barnung; but the blinds of his consulting room were always down, and no one seemed to have heard of him. I tried in vain to get into the building which, in times gone by, I'd known like the back of my hand, and had myself manhandled by the guards for my pains; the nurses shrugged their shoulders at my questions and assumed a distant air when I approached the reception desk, giving me perfunctory or irritated answers and refusing to summon the false Frau Goldstein when I asked to speak to her.

My run-down appearance was hardly in my favour: I had a long beard, my hair was dishevelled and my clothes filthy beyond belief. I walked with a limp, dragging my right foot; livid with cold, my hands shook like those of a man with palsy. But at least I no longer had to hide myself when my throat tightened and I began to caw and hiss; indeed, my convulsions were most effective in gaining me the sympathy of the passers-by, who would never have suspected me of faking such spasms. However eager they might be to catch their trains, commuters turned pale at the sight of me gibbering away on my bit of cardboard; they threw down generous handfuls of coins and moved off, looking worried. There was a faint scent of spring in the air and even the rain had a different smell, of freshly tilled earth and grass, but the nights were still cold.

The police wouldn't allow me to sleep in the warm near the vents in the underground, or in an underpass, so I slept by day, in a more or less upright position on the ballast near the railway station. As soon as they saw me beginning to loll against the wall, a truncheon would be pressed into action and the policeman on duty would send me packing. At times when I knew they would be there, I would drag myself to the ticket-office and on to the relevant platform to look at the trains to Geneva, peer at the busy attendants through the windows of the wagons-lit, at the inspectors with their red shoulder straps, and at the first luggage-laden passengers; scanning their quintessentially Swiss faces, I felt like hugging them, telling them that I was every bit as Swiss as they were, and that I wanted to go home. But right from the first days when I'd taken up residence in the station my eye had been caught by the Geneva dailies on the news-stand, with my photograph on the front page, and the headlines of Romanian papers translated into French. I was a wanted person even in my own land. The story of the blameless high-ranking civil servant turned assassin and bandit was everywhere. I was cornered, and sometimes I felt like giving myself up, going to die peacefully in a cell, allowing myself to be sentenced to hard labour without even bothering to explain what had happened to me. I would be taken care of, looked after; I would have company, perhaps even sympathy. But I couldn't die without knowing who had killed Stauber, what had happened to Ortega and the others, where Dr. Barnung was hiding and how the interpreter was involved in this whole business.

At first they threatened violence, but they ended up by putting up with me. I didn't touch any of their things, I didn't put a foot in the basement, with its piles of sand and gravel, I didn't ever go up to the floors where they lived and slept, in gangs. I kept myself to myself in the concrete space beneath the stairs, hidden behind a wall of cardboard, together with my rags. I'd only go there when it was getting dark, and by dawn I'd be out again, to avoid meeting them. With time, though, the squatters became used to my presence, and sometimes brought me food, which they said they got for almost nothing from the markets on Friday evenings; they'd unload crates of fruit from their van, bags of bread, eggs and even meat, which they'd cook and share out amongst themselves in front of a bonfire in the basement. There was also a lot of beer, and by the end of these sessions someone would always be flat on their back in the sand, the worse for wear. On certain evenings other gangs would join them, and the atmosphere would gradually become heated: a threatening buzz would spread through the unfinished building, down the dark staircases, through the bare echoing rooms and empty corridors. The squatters would unearth sticks and cudgels, start wielding bottles and jerry cans, rummage around in the darkness filling rucksacks with bolts. Every now and again one would let out a bloodcurdling whoop, a sort of war cry to incite the rest. I'd peek at them through a gap in the cardboard; their heads swathed in black handkerchiefs, they'd leave the building in small groups, then vanish into the dark streets, among the glistening cars and rubbish bins, to come back at dawn, silent and exhausted. Through the smoky glow I could just make out their dim figures as they took off their disguises and hid their weapons under the piles of gravel. Then they'd disperse, as mysteriously as they had come, and when the first glimmer of dawn appeared, lighting up the bare concrete pillars, you would never have known that anyone had been there at all.

One night, there must have been about fifty of them sitting outside my cardboard den, but this time they weren't preparing for an expedition; they didn't have any weapons, they weren't distributing bottles and bolts. They were just smoking, in silence, the tips of their cigarettes weaving in the dark. Someone threw a handful of gravel against my cardboard, asking me whether I wanted a smoke; the others laughed and called out more or less in unison:

'Hey, Swissman! Come on out, there's some really good stuff tonight!'

Afraid of offending them, I got up and went out hesitantly to join them – I didn't really know any of them at all, for me they were just nameless faces in a tight-knit pack. But I did know some of their voices: the one who had called me had always seemed well-disposed towards me, right from the start he had made sure the others left me alone. I'd listened in horror from behind my cardboard as he'd managed to dissuade his companions from setting it on fire. So I followed his voice and went to sit next to him; he passed me a cigarette I'd no desire to smoke, but I took a puff anyway and handed it back to him.

At that same moment, two yellow lights appeared in the space outside the building and lit up the squatters' faces; then a large car appeared and stopped just in front of the concrete pillars, its headlights pointing at the ceiling. The back window was rolled down and a pale face peered out for a moment, only to be hurriedly withdrawn. The squatters extinguished their cigarettes and put them into their pockets; they got up from the heaps of gravel and went to stand in a line next to the car. One by one, they filed past the car window, from which a white hand passed them something, though I couldn't make out what. Then they came back towards the building and went silently back up the stairs, or off along the street in small groups. I was now the only person left in the semi-basement; seated on my heap of gravel, I stared at the car headlights, shielding my eyes with my hands. After a few moments the door opened and I saw a tall, smartly dressed man coming slowly towards me, picking his way among the puddles, his hands in his pockets.

'I see you're not one of them, then,' he said, looking at me curiously; he sat down on the low concrete wall outside the semi-basement and carried on staring at me appraisingly.

'I come here at night, to shelter,' I told him, somewhat mortified.

'And may I ask you what brings you to this god-forsaken spot?' There was something kindly about his tone; I stood up, made awkward by his gentle manner – for too long now I'd had dealings only with riff-raff.

'Needs must… I sleep in there,' I said, pointing my chin in the direction of my cardboard abode.

'If I'm not mistaken, you're not from round here. French, perhaps?'

'Not really. Swiss,' I gently corrected him.

'Swiss?' he repeated in some amusement. 'You must be the only Swiss vagrant on the face of the earth. Don't tell me you used to be a banker!'

I shook my head and lowered my eyes from the dazzling headlights at which I'd been staring so fixedly. The man gestured to his chauffeur, who turned both the lights and the engine off; now the dim parking lights were the only source of illumination amidst so much darkness. All that could be heard were the usual night noises; the squatters' footsteps were receding, together with the clang of their boots as they hit the odd metal bin.

'They come and eat out of my hand!' said the man, turning his head towards the road and getting up from the wall.

'That's my contribution to saving the world!' he added, laughing. He took a few steps backward, turned away from me and looked up at the sky.

'Have you been with them for long?' he asked, raising his voice so that I could hear him.

'A week or so,' I answered vaguely. He turned back towards me, sinking his feet in the gravel, which crunched beneath his soles.

'Well... can I offer you a drink?'

'Thank you. But I don't know whether...'

'Oh, don't worry, we'll soon get that sorted out!' he said cheerfully as the chauffeur switched on the engine.

I emerged from the semi-basement, shaking off the worst of the filth from my clothing, and sat down nervously on the edge of the soft leather seat.

V

Klaus Burke was one of the richest men in Munich; he owned various businesses making a wide range of products, from taps to engine filters, windscreens and plumbing equipment.

'To tell the truth, I don't even know how many I've got, or where they are; some of them I've never even seen. I don't know anything about what I produce; I just move money around on the stock exchange, or rather, my managing director does that for me,' he admitted in the grand restaurant he'd brought me to. First though, we'd gone to his elegant apartment in the city centre, where I'd been able to have a hot bath and change my clothes. Taking off my rags and sinking into the scented foam, I'd had my first sight of my body for quite some time. With a sense of deep relief I massaged my roughened, parchment-yellow skin, leaving my hands to soak in the hot water to alleviate the cramp in my fingers. Scarcely able to believe my luck, I buttoned up the warm woollen jacket and ran my hands luxuriously over my stubble-free cheeks. Almost dizzy with pleasure, I gloried in the warmth of the radiators and the softness of the armchair when I finally rejoined Klaus Burke in the drawing room.

'I use this apartment for business meetings with my clients and directors, but I don't live here; I prefer to be in my villa on the Ammersee, among my horses and my woods,' my host informed me as he showed me around.

The windows had a view of the cathedral spires, soaring above the city lights. Running his hands through his thick white hair in front of the mirror, Burke straightened his black tie and added:

'You can be my guest there if you like. The Ammersee is lovely at this time of year – the storks will soon be back, and everything is white with hawthorn.'

At the restaurant I'd sipped slowly at the *bisque de homard*, allowing its warmth to penetrate my every fibre, almost weeping as I savoured the fine French wine. I was no longer used to eating, and couldn't manage very much. My life, I realised, had been reduced to a minimum, but a tiny flame still flickered within me and now it was being kindled anew. My appetite was slowly coming back, my blood was flowing more strongly through my veins; my body was shuffling off its listlessness and, as it did so, I could feel my mad desire to track down the interpreter regaining strength. In fact, it had never entirely left me; it was a physical need, a call which was reasserting itself and demanding to be obeyed.

Klaus Burke drew deeply on his Havana cigar and looked at me through the smoke.

'You may wonder why a man like me should bother spending his time giving money to those down-and-outs.' I nodded distractedly, my body tensing in sudden fear of an imminent convulsion. My host paused for a moment, lost in thought, then carried on:

'You see, most men get through their lives as best they can, and no one expects anything more of them. But then there are people like us; some inscrutable higher power has decreed that we have a mission on this earth!'

I jumped, feeling he'd read my thoughts, but my host continued imperturbably:

'Ever since I first set foot in a factory, aged eleven, everything I've touched has turned to gold. The wealth just piles up – I'm the living embodiment of the German economic miracle. Every enterprise I've embarked on has flourished, each brand I've invested in has multiplied ten, a hundred, a thousand-fold. I've discovered markets no one had dreamed of, invented others which seemed to have no *raison d'être*, created absurd desires and satisfied them with my factories. Success is my default setting. Yet I myself was born of ruination: I am a child of wretchedness, of a death so harrowing it knows no solace. I carried my mother's charred body through the streets during the bombing of Hamburg. My father has been dead for sixty years, and yet I see him still: at Hamburg University, in a jar of formalin in the faculty of natural sciences. His right eye is still open, and under the three day's growth of beard you can still see the bluish mark I made when I embraced him with inky fingers, as the English planes began to bomb the city.'

He tapped the ash off his cigar and paused for a few moments, looking at me with a solemn, thoughtful expression. I sensed that he was weighing up the words he was about to speak.

'I wanted to escape the rubble of the Hamburg streets, where the charred remains of men and animals and buildings lay mingled in a single clammy mush; I wanted to put the unquenchable flames of those fearful nights out of my mind. I wanted to redeem myself, to win, to build – in a word, I wanted to forget. But destruction seeks me out, stirs up a mocking yearning for the death I have escaped. For sixty years I've been repaying fate for the price of my survival, but nothing will suffice to rid me of my guilt, and I'm too base to go back alone to the pit out of which I've climbed. So I assuage my remorse by paying those desperadoes to shatter the windscreens I produce, to set fire to my supermarkets; that way at least some portion of me will be destroyed. Let them hammer away, break bones, smash windows, wreck the city! I gain reassurance from their empty futures, their desperation, the death they carry with them. They leave open the door for me – for my return.'

So saying, Klaus Burke shook himself, as though a shiver had run down his spine; his expression suddenly distant and cold, he continued sitting there stock-still, almost as though he'd lost consciousness, then began to breathe heavily. Beads of sweat pearled on his forehead and he started blinking rapidly. Then he regained his composure, beckoned the waiter with a flick of his wrist and ordered a cognac; only after he'd taken a few sips did his breathing return to normal.

'I am seeking a death that is worthy of me, Mr. Bellamy. I can't resign myself to dying in my bed, eaten up by cancer or old age. Nor do I want to yield to the lure of some elaborately-planned suicide. I want to die with a curse upon my lips, to re-experience the horror of that summer's night. Only that way will I have paid my dues; only that way will I be free. Such is my mission!'

He balanced his cigar on the edge of the ashtray, straightened up in his armchair, placed his hands around his glass and leant towards me:

'And you, dear friend – what form of destruction are you after?'

I told him my story; puffing on his cigar as he heard me out, Klaus Burke seemed both incredulous and amused. I showed him the Romanian newspaper cuttings about the robberies, the interpreter's list, and Stauber's too, with the four mysterious handwritten names, I showed him Tibor Preda's passport with my photograph. I described the therapies used in Dr. Barnung's clinic and my chilling discovery of the whistling men in Odessa. When at last I fell silent, my host sighed deeply and looked at me with new respect.

'Mr. Bellamy, I'm full of admiration! If there were a museum of incredible destinies, yours would be worthy of a place of honour; and, may I say, I cannot imagine any other man confronting such adversities with anything like your courage and tenacity!'

I felt flattered. I had received many compliments during the course of my life – on my commitment to study, on my capacity for hard work – but never before had I been praised for my sheer ill-fortune. Thinking over Klaus Burke's words, I realised that I had indeed become a museum piece, or rather perhaps a fairground curiosity, a freak to be exhibited as a warning to those who do not believe in the wayward power of fate.

'But you must take me to this clinic, Mr. Bellamy! I'll have myself admitted – I too would like to be subjected to his diabolical experiments!' Burke said excitedly.

'I don't think there's anything left of Dr. Barnung here in Munch; I've been to look for him in his clinic on several occasions. There's no longer any sign of the patients who were there with me; they must all have become whistling men, locked up in some god-forsaken madhouse!'

My host looked disappointed; he flicked at his cigar and sat there in silence, watching the wreath of smoke as it spiralled upwards through the air.

Over the days that followed, Burke entertained me royally at his villa on the Ammersee, showed me his paintings and the valuable antiquarian books he had in his library. We visited the stud farm where he bred racing horses, and went hunting on the large estate he owned on the lake's edge. The woods, the green meadows, the view of distant blue mountains, the quiet, familiar waters of the lake – all were a balm to my troubled spirit. As if by a miracle, the sky cleared and a weak sun emerged to warm the cold, damp earth. The delicate colours of the countryside, the long periods of sleep in which I could now indulge, the unfamiliar landscape, all gave me the impression that I was observing the world from a safe and peaceful haven. The tender light of spring returned, lingering to the west on the bark of trees now tinged with green, on the stone walls of distant farms. In the morning I would look out of the window to see the dawn light merging with the lake, reflected rose-pink in the network of canals, and I would imagine that I could see the white ferryboat plying the waters of another lake, I could even hear its hooter, and the muffled sound of summer music. I would stare fixedly at that tranquil scene until the sun, rising behind the trees, dispelled the fleeting mirage with the dazzle of its rays.

One afternoon, coming in after a walk, I found Burke in the living-room, sitting in front of an open fire.

'My dear Bellamy, did you see that sunset? And the sky full of birds, too, and the beeches positively bursting into leaf. It's incredible how nature is so set on coming to life again!' he exclaimed, walking over to the bay window overlooking the park. 'And how are you feeling today? I see you've been out for a walk.'

'I felt a bit dizzy this morning, but I'm fine now, thank you. Now though, if you don't mind, I need to take the weight off my feet,' I said, collapsing heavily on to the divan.

'Please, of course, make yourself at home! Would you like a drink? A cup of tea, perhaps?'

I nodded in thanks and my host nodded to the butler, who left the room and returned shortly afterwards with a tea tray, which he placed before me; Burke, on the other hand, was presented with a small glass containing a colourless liquid.

'I myself am having something stronger,' he said apologetically, holding the little glass bubble up in front of the flickering flames; he rose to his feet and went to lean against the chimneybreast, loosening his silk scarf as he did so. He stood there in silence for some minutes, staring at the pattern in the carpet at his feet.

'Mr. Bellamy, I'd like to tell you in all sincerity that you can be my guest here for as long as you like – your presence takes my mind off certain dark thoughts, and your unexpected company lightens my dull existence. I can see that this rest on the Ammersee is doing you good – you're regaining your physical strength, and you seem more inwardly peaceful, too. But if you want to set off on your quest again – to continue with your pursuit – well, I'd be only too happy to give you such help as I can,' said Burke, striking a more serious note. He sipped his drink and put his glass down on the marble slab.

'I'm very grateful to you for all your hospitality and kindness. After all that I've been through, here at last I've been able to find a bit of peace of mind. But I think that the best thing for me now is to go back to Geneva. I'm tired, I'm not well and I no longer have the strength to carry on with my mission. All in all, ending my days in a Swiss prison wouldn't be so bad. Don't worry about me, Mr. Burke, somehow or other I'll get by. But I'm afraid I'll have to ask you for a bit of money for the journey,' I said, lowering my eyes in embarrassment. My host was walking to and fro in front of the fire, hand on hip. Now he stooped to pick up his glass.

'Mr. Bellamy, I have a proposal to put to you, and I beg you not to be shocked at my brutality. By now you will have realised that I regard charitable impulses as unnatural. If there is a God, I'm certain he has not put me in this world to do good, but rather to foster the memory of the evil which lies at the root of my being, even if, in fact, I myself could not be said to have suffered as a consequence of it. These are my childhood memories, and what is more sacred than a childhood memory? Now, despite the fact that I'm no believer in good works, I'll gladly give you the money you need to get back to Switzerland; furthermore, should you want me to, I can find you the best lawyers, and with a bit of luck I'm sure that they'll be able to keep you out of prison. But I must confess that what particularly interests me is your mission, your pursuit of the whistling interpreter and the mysterious language clinic. Behind this story I sense the fires of destruction lurking, the destruction of which I was born. All in all, I too would be sorry if you gave up the chase right now, after having embarked on it with such doggedness. So I am proposing that we make a deal: I am prepared to finance your quest for as long as it may take – provided you let me come with you, that you afford me the privilege of being there when you catch up with your interpreter, when we discover the consequences of Dr. Barnung's dastardly experiments, and the madhouse with the whistling men!' He was fixing me with a positively diabolical expression as he spoke; he picked up his glass and threw the contents into the hearth; the fire sputtered and spat out blue flames.

That same evening, while I was getting ready for bed, I was seized by one of the most devastating convulsions I'd experienced so far, one which included phenomena I'd never previously noted. Now my arms were trembling, as well as my legs; my fingers splayed and held close to my chest, I found that I was banging my elbows against my sides, emitting long whistles from deep in my throat. These in their turn were interspersed by rapid gurgling sounds, which gradually subsided, only to dissolve into uninterrupted blethering the moment I could relax my jaws and loosen my tongue. Now for the first time it was clear to me that the gestures my body was trapped into making were reminiscent of the animal-like movements of the whistling men I'd seen in the convent in Odessa. So now there was no getting round it: I too was on the point of becoming one of those monsters. The attack ended with confused jabberings not unlike those that can be heard on an old gramophone record played at the wrong speed. Oddly enough, it seemed to me that those mysterious, fragmentary words had meaning, belonged to some language. They weren't Romanian, though they resembled it; strangulated, thrust back into my throat by a series of violent cramps, they struck familiar notes, ones which my lips seemed somehow accustomed to uttering. Hearing my ravings, Burke had come running into my room, but was at a loss as to what to do; he went to get me a glass of water, tried to help me up from the floor, but after a bit all he could do was look on helplessly, waiting to see what would happen. When the spasm passed, he helped me to sit up.

'Mr. Bellamy, this is a godsend! I realise now that I would never have understood anything about your problem had I not been present at this chilling demonstration of it. You may find my interest morbid and cruel, but you must concede that all this is quite fascinating. I have witnessed your brain rebelling against its normal function and shaking around in your cranium in search of a different way of being, as though it were contracting, trying to regain a shape it had lost, but not forgotten! I imagine you've never been able to see yourself in such a state, but I was watching you carefully just now, and frightening thoughts came into my mind. Because, you see, the changes that came over you, your grimaces, the way your shoulders twisted and your hands spread out, all gave me the feeling that your organism was not fighting the whiplash of disease, but rather answering some compelling summons, some powerful yearning to assume a different bodily form. Your eyes were like those of a lizard, your neck was twitching like that of a bird and you were flapping your arms like wings, thrusting out your chest and floundering around on the floor with your feet together. Your first whistle was very faint, almost imperceptible; it swelled to an eagle's cry, then sunk to a monkey's syncopated chatter, finally to become a jumble of apparently intelligible sounds linked to each other in unintelligible ways. What I was seeing, Mr. Bellamy, was nothing less than a synthesis of evolution.'

Still breathless and exhausted by my spasms, I gave my host a weary glance, too worn out even to express my irritation at his words; I closed my eyes, wiping the sweat from my face with my shirt sleeve. With a mute wave of my still trembling hand, I asked for water; Burke proffered me the glass, then went to get a towel and bent down to wipe my forehead.

'Forgive me, Mr. Bellamy,' he murmured without looking at me.

We left Munich one morning in late May. The chauffeur was waiting for us with the engine running; Burke had him load a large suitcase into the car, and I wondered what on earth could be in it. We boarded a plane for Berlin, then carried on to Vilnius, where we spent the night. The next morning we hired a car and drove on towards Klaipeda; the road ran through gentle wooded hills, and we had a sky full of motionless white clouds above us throughout the journey.

Klaipeda is a white city which rises sharply out of the sand, opening up at the sea's edge into a mesh of straight roads, with a narrow spit of land in front of it which then broadens out to the south, trapping a branch of the sea; and that imprisoned sea looks somehow solidified there among the sands, it has a dead gleam to it, revealing its nakedness, the scaly skin of its depths, the strips of tiny shells which run across it like the exhausted veins of some former seam of precious metal. Two of the best rooms in the most luxurious hotel in town awaited us; the vast expanse of open sea visible through the light-filled windows gave me a sense of weariness. I glanced at my rucksack on the bed, at the new clothes Burke had bought for me, and felt myself doubly a prisoner. My benefactor, on the other hand, was clearly ever more exhilarated by the prospect of the chase; that night at dinner he ordered champagne to celebrate our undertaking.

'So where shall we begin, Mr. Bellamy? It's you who must now take over the reins!' he said excitedly, raising his foaming glass.

We signed up for an intensive course in Lithuanian, put on in Klaipeda by the University of Vilnius. My heart was beating hard as we entered the lecture hall on the ground floor of a small building by the sea; an usher was arranging the seats and laying green folders on the desks. The first row was occupied by a group of silent Africans, all wearing track suits and peering around with a bewildered air. Burke and I took our places at the back of the hall, both of us with our eyes on the main door.

'Have you ever attended a course in a foreign language before, Mr. Burke?' I asked him as I leafed through the folder.

'Only a bit of business English. Languages have never been my forte. I feel a bit of a clown when I try to talk English; I fear that no one is going to take me seriously. It reminds me of when I was a child and would put on my mother's clothes as a joke, and look at myself in the mirror and shudder.'

'You'll see – you're bound to learn something even without trying!' I told him kindly, feeling myself to be something of an authority on the subject.

A group of boys now sauntered in, with a listless air about them; they sat down in front of us and immediately took out their mobile phones. Shortly afterwards two stiff-looking women appeared in the doorway, looking as if they knew it all; then four gaudily-dressed Asian men drifted in, one after the other, with business-like rucksacks from which they extracted mineral-water bottles, coloured pens and large exercise-books which they laid out neatly on their desks. The last person to come through the door, with a confident, bouncing step, was the teacher herself, a portly middle-aged woman with red hair and clear skin; she sat down heavily at the teacher's desk, slipped off her shoes and started calling out our names, peering at us from over her glasses and flaring her nostrils, as though she hoped that this would keep them in place. She handed out sheets of paper with various illustrations, and started off by having us pronounce short sentences and ask each other questions; we had to look at the images and link them to one of the words that she was repeating. Burke looked somewhat out of his depth; he made matters worse for himself by trying to guess his question in advance.

'Mr. Bellamy, are you sure that all this is necessary?' he whispered to me.

'I don't know, Mr. Burke. But if the interpreter has indeed been through Klaipeda, it will certainly have been to learn Lithuanian. Just be patient, something will come of it, you'll see.'

When we got back to the hotel that first afternoon we were hungry and exhausted; after a bite to eat, I lay down on the bed and slept till evening, while Burke doggedly did his homework.

'I can't help myself, Mr. Bellamy – I have to succeed, even in this. Klaus Burke is doomed to excel, he has to come first. You'll see – I'll get top marks!'

Klaipeda was a soporific place. The leaden expanse of sea gave me a feeling of security; I gave myself over to its protective embrace, but somewhere inside me lurked the feeling that its placid presence might conceal some hidden threat. In the quiet afternoons when I was asleep, with the flat, cold light coming in through the windows, I would dream that the sea too would come in and lap round the foot of my bed. I would wake up with a start, seized by an irrational fear of drowning. At that dead hour of the day, streets and houses seemed on the point of fading away into nothingness, becoming incorporeal. Towards evening the wind would get up, blowing in from the open sea, setting flags and sails snapping; the surface of the water would shatter into sharp little dark waves, which would come to shore as though they were made of oil, without tang or foam. The light, too, would change: the air would become tinged with yellow, things would lose further definition and dissolve into a quivering mirage. The sand would be whipped up from the beach and spin around in the wind, to land on pavements, cars, balconies, café awnings, beating against windows, bleaching the leaves on the trees. It was as though the whole city were about to be slowly engulfed under one vast sand-dune and was patiently accepting its fate. Dusk was already gathering when I went down into the foyer, to find Burke poring over his books.

'Mr. Bellamy, did you know that Lithuanian is one of Europe's oldest languages, the last remains of the time when the Baltic and Slav languages merged? It seems that Lithuanian is the language closest to that of the Indo-Europeans. Apparently linguists regard it as being directly related to Hittite!' he said excitedly, pointing to the thick volume he'd got from the local library.

'That shows we're on the right track,' I answered, still half-asleep, then flopped down on to the chair next to him.

After a week, we decided to go our separate ways; Burke would carry on with the course and I would snoop around town. I also went to the town library and looked through the list of who had borrowed what, I hung around in the reading room of the foreign languages section to see who came in and out, I struck up conversations with the librarians in search of the slightest clue that might confirm the interpreter's presence in the place. I checked the hotels, giving princely tips to the porters so that they'd give me the names of all the foreigners who'd stayed there over the previous month, but all to no avail. The course ended, Burke passed the exam for beginners' Lithuanian with flying colours, but there was still no sign of the interpreter. We made one last attempt by putting an advert in a local paper, asking for a simultaneous interpreter whose mother tongue was Lithuanian but who would be working in a combination of French, German and Lithuanian. On the day it appeared in the *Nasza Gazeta* we stayed in the hotel from dawn to dusk, vainly awaiting a call.

That night I slept very fitfully; I had the feeling I was suffocating, and opened the windows several times to air the room. The sky was dark and starless; a heavy mist was advancing slowly over the sea, spreading into the streets and covering everything with what looked like heavy dew. Towards dawn, a huge cruise ship sailed silently past the town and berthed in the harbour at the end of the bay, the thousand lights of its decks reflected brokenly at the water's edge, sending a watery dazzle over the walls of my room. I went back to bed and, after much tossing and turning, fell into a troubled sleep. I thought I heard someone fiddling with the handle of the door, and tried to arouse myself from my drowsiness to go and check, but then decided it was just another of my hallucinations and went back to sleep.

The dawn light was at last filtering in through the shadows of my tousled sheets, my head ached, my eyes were burning; my breathing was heavy and laboured. I decided to get dressed and go and get a breath of air. The hotel was still sunk in sleep; the lift was standing empty at the top floor, its light falling gloomily on the wall. I eavesdropped outside Burke's door and was about to knock, but decided not to wake him and took the stairs. The restaurant was still in darkness, but the foyer smelled of smoke and liquor. I breathed in the damp, salty outside air with a sense of relief, then crossed the road and went to the jetty where the cruise ship was moored. The funnels were still smoking, and deep in the depths of its iron hulk I could hear distant engines throbbing. A lone lorry was shunting around, its headlamps slicing through the violet air; a few shivering passengers were already on the deck of the cruise ship, watching the outline of the city gradually emerging from the mist. But suddenly, rather than clearing, it became thicker; a salty wind blew in from the sea, and the city was enveloped in ragged spray. I retraced my steps and went absent-mindedly down to the beach rather than back to the hotel. I could hear the waves lapping gently on the shore; I went down the steps and let my feet sink into the sand. In the distance I could just make out the vague outline of the landing-stages at the tourist harbour; rather than floating, the boats rose out of the glassy water as though they were somehow attached to the sea floor, their masts oozing plump drops which fell almost silently on to the deck. I walked down to the waterline and stamped my feet in the wake of a lingering wave, sinking my stick into the sand to see how firm it was and leaving deep, soft footprints, then watching them disappear as the water swept over them.

It was then that I saw them, like a mirage: a few metres from the shore, half-sunk in a muddy pool, lay dozens of black narwhals, their spiral tusks pointing towards the sky. Some were twitching their tails, others lay there motionless, as though dead. I left my shoes on the sand and waded towards them, thigh-deep in water. In the meantime, other people too had become aware of their mysterious presence, and were running in the same direction. Now I was standing right by their huge, wrinkled, shell-incrusted bodies. They did not seem at all alarmed: they looked at me sadly with their moist eyes, moving their upper jaws set, like a nose, with their single pointed tusk. A silent crowd had gathered on the shore, but few people actually approached the creatures. One of those who did was an elderly man with a thin red beard, who was wearing waders; he was considering the scene with a sorrowful air.

'Are you a foreigner?' he asked me in German, staring at the elegant windcheater with which Burke had provided me.

I nodded.

'This is the third time this has happened this spring. No one knows how they come to land up here; they don't come from around these parts, yet dozens of them end up stranded here,' he said, extending his arms in a puzzled gesture.

'Will they die?' I asked.

'A few will survive until the turn of the tide, but they clearly suffer from being stuck here; they wave their tusks around and moan piteously – you can hear them right in the centre of town. But yes, most of them will die. Then the waves bring them ashore; they get stuck in the sand, like great black stones, and have to be carted away by bulldozers, because they make a terrible stench,' he said with a look of utter disgust. I followed him towards the shore, dragging my feet in the sand.

'The strange thing is, they're all male; only the males have that tusk. And they're all young; it's as though a whole generation had lost its sense of direction and started wandering through the Baltic, looking for a way out towards the Arctic!' He paused, as though pondering the matter.

'They're not afraid of humans; they let themselves be touched,' he went on; going up to one of them, he drew his hand over the dark skin of its back, sheathed in a layer of glittering sand. The narwhal gave a weary shake of its tail, lifted its tusk and sunk back into the stagnant shallows.

'Have you seen them fight?'

I shook my head.

'They clash their tusks together like sabres and fight endless duels. I've caught them at it on occasions, in the ice floes, outlined against the rose-pink wall of the arctic ice, when there's no wind and it's never dark – it's a rare sight. They heave themselves out of the water black as pitch, and in that endless silence you can hear their tusks rattling like branches in the wind!'

I looked towards the throng of animals, now vanishing into the mist; some of them had ceased moving, and were gradually sinking into the sand.

'Can you smell that smell? They smell of seaweed, of the depths; of a cold, dark world where man has never set foot!' he went on, staring at me with an expression I could not fathom. Then he waved me a mournful goodbye and wandered towards the creatures furthest off, at the far side of the shallows; feeling they had sufficient water around them to make a getaway, they were flinging themselves this way and that, leaping about frantically in their efforts to reach the open sea.

Cold and bedraggled, I plodded up the beach, then sat down and rubbed my numb feet before putting on my shoes. A sudden burst of blinding sunlight pierced through the mist, lighting up the doomed landscape with a surreal gleam; floating there on the hushed surface, the narwhals took on the appearance of one single, gigantic beast, its back bristling with barbs. As though it had registered this similarity, the crowd on the beach let out a unanimous gasp; the shells embedded in the creatures' skin now caught the glancing light and sparkled like shards of glass; even the damp sand lit up in a fitful glitter.

I hurried back to the hotel; I wanted to wake Burke up and take him to see the beached narwhals. But there was a message for me from him at the reception desk:

'Mr. Bellamy, this morning someone called about our ad, a certain Mirko Stolojan. I've agreed to meet him at ten. If you want to join us, this is the address: Perkelos Gatve 40, Klaipeda. The porter tells me it's a road somewhere near the port. See you later,
     K. Burke.

Still stiff with cold and bewildered by the message, I stared idiotically at the porter, who in his turn was giving me a puzzled look.

'What time is it?' I asked out of the blue.

'A quarter past ten. Breakfast is over, but we could still serve you some coffee,' he hastened to assure me, as though he could read my thoughts. I folded up the note and leant wearily against the counter; nothing would have been more welcome than a cup of hot coffee, its smell wafting towards me from the jugs on the trolley by the window. I was hungry and tired from my long walk; I could have sat down in the foyer and waited quietly for Burke's return. But my head was spinning, as I now had another worry.

'Is there anything wrong, sir?' enquired the doorman solicitously.

'No, everything's fine,' I said distractedly, then ran out of the foyer and leapt into the first of the taxis parked in front of the hotel.

Perkelos Gatve was a quiet residential road which began just beyond the mouth of the harbour canal, below the last cranes in the goods yard, to continue along the coast and on into the woods. No. 40 was a small villa with an unfenced garden, set back a little from the road; it was surrounded by an unkempt lawn dotted with thorny bushes, sloping gently down to the shore. I waited for the taxi to drive off, then walked up the sandy path to the door, which was on the right side of the house; I rang the bell, but there was no answer. Total silence, except for a rustling of leaves. After a few minutes, I rang again, then went to peer in through the small window which gave on to the street, but all I could see was a dark wooden chest-of-drawers and a divan upholstered in some pale material. I checked Burke's message – I was at the right address. I inspected the back of the house, the side facing the sea, where there was a tradesmen's entrance; I knocked and found it was open, so I went in.

'Is anyone at home?' I called, and immediately found myself in the living-room I'd seen through the window. It was furnished like the cabin of a ship, with brass lamps hanging from brightly painted beams and gleaming door handles. All in apple-pie order; not a speck of dust. It smelled of ammonia and well-oiled rope; a clock in a copper case ticked on the chest of drawers. In the kitchen I heard the buzz of a fridge; I opened the door – it was empty, but immaculate. I went back into the living-room, which was dimly lit by such light as made its way in through a little port-hole of coloured glass. A wooden staircase led to the upper floor; the handrail and banisters were carved with elaborate motifs connected to the sea, and small glass cases containing weirdly-shaped shells hung from the wooden walls. I went up cautiously and found myself in a large studio which took up the whole floor, the end wall occupied by a nautical chart of the Baltic Sea; on a console table between the two windows stood a small model of a sailing ship bearing the Polish flag. Behind a table strewn with books and maps, almost the whole of the opposite wall was occupied by a sophisticated sound system; I was intrigued by the two large spools, placed behind a glass panel, and the sound boxes, protected by thick chunks of foam. The only remaining empty space, I noticed, was occupied by a document set in a gold frame, which proved to be a diploma – awarded by the University of Heidelberg to Mirko Stolojan, a simultaneous translator whose languages were Russian, Latvian and Lithuanian. Overcome by sudden weariness, I sat down in the leather armchair in front of the sound system. I was sweating profusely, though from exhaustion rather than emotion, and my throat was strangely dry. Through the porthole I could see the dark mass of water, heaving like a slab of steel, sending ripples of white light over the walls of the room. Since it was right there in front of my nose, I pressed the button on the sound system, setting the spools in motion. At first it gave out a dry whirring noise, then the sound of waves on the sea shore and distant engines; then suddenly there was a voice, perfectly loud and clear. I recognised it – it was that of the interpreter, speaking in German, in the typically distant tone adopted by such professionals. I noted the awkward way the sentences were stitched together, the tail ends left loose, then suddenly if clumsily tidied up and made to fit together. Another voice was audible in the background, probably that of the original speaker, but I couldn't make out what language he was talking; the words seemed to me short, three syllables at most, with the stress on the penultimate. He must have acquired it relatively recently if he had such trouble translating it. I carried on listening, and then I heard his voice changing, becoming deeper and taking on a syncopated rhythm, with mangled single syllables and incomprehensible combinations of diphthongs. Then I recognised the wheezing, rasping, gurgling sounds given out by the uvula when the throat muscles become constricted. If in some ways similar, those sounds were also different from those which I myself produced when I was having one of my convulsions. I thought the effort involved might have explained the difference. I listened on, until the sound lost all resemblance to any human voice and became just a whistle, rising and falling, elusive and mysterious. I saw him in my mind as he had been that last time by the lake, and it occurred to me to wonder whether indeed that tape might have been recorded in that very place, on just such a wild night. I wound back the spool and put on another, then another; all they contained were whistling, lowing sounds, a slow repeated twittering interspersed with a low buzz. No trace of a human voice; as though he had ceased to speak once and for all, and was now simply howling.

I left Mirko Stolojan's house on foot; it was not yet two o'clock, but already the sun was going down, and thick white mist was rolling in from the sea, settling over the shoreline but stopping at the woods. Anchored at the edge of the bay, the cruise ship was now nothing more than a ghostly, shapeless presence. A siren hooted in the distance and the harbour lights started flashing. Suddenly seized with a burst of panic, I stumbled through the pebble-strewn sand, but the effort caused my head to swim and I had to pause for a moment on the grass. In the goods yard I at last found a taxi to take me back to the hotel, where I found the foyer in a state of uproar; people were talking at the tops of their voices, and the smoke was as thick as the mist outside. Seated on the sofas, several photographers were fiddling with their cameras; a reporter was heaving his cine camera on to his shoulder. Seeing me coming in, the porter gestured at me in alarm from behind his desk. I was about to go over to him, when I found myself surrounded by black-uniformed police. Cameras flashed, photographers clustered round me, jockeying for position; I could hardly breathe. I tried to fight my way towards a chair, but a man with fleshy pink lips burst through the cordon of policemen and pushed his way towards me threateningly, grabbing me by the elbow and dragging me into the manager's office.

'Are you Mr. Tibor Preda?' he asked in German, leafing through my passport.

'That's me,' I lied.

'Inspector Zabukas, border police.' He handed me back my passport and clasped his hands behind his back.

'Mr. Preda, I must ask you to come with me,' he said in a solemn tone, summoning two other policemen with a flick of his fingers. I allowed myself to be led out without a struggle, already thinking of new headlines in the Swiss and Romanian papers. I'd be back on the front page with a new photograph, the new clean-shaven face of the Beast of Bukovina, this time with handcuffs on. I would inspire new editorials, crowds of journalists would be waiting for me at Bucharest. I'd see Magda again – in a courtroom. They'd question us, try us and sentence us; in the dark confines of some god-forsaken prison, they might even rough us up – out of sheer rage, by way of punishment, to make us confess to other crimes we didn't commit. I'd end up in some stinking cell where, stricken with illness and brought low by violent treatment, I might find death at last. It was better that way; that was how things should end.

We left the office and went out into the street, dodging the photographers who were waiting for us in the foyer; the man with fleshy lips was walking beside me, with the policemen following. We crossed the road and walked towards the sea. I wondered what our final destination would be; I was expecting to be bundled into a police car and driven off to the police station, sirens blaring, but instead we were walking down the beach. The mist was thicker than ever, and everything was enveloped in the early darkness; the outlines of the narwhals were still just visible in the dark water, though there seemed to be fewer of them. I wondered whether some of them might have managed to make it into the open sea, borne off on the outgoing tide. The man with fleshy lips was walking straight towards them. A wooden footbridge had been laid on the shore, spanning the pool and reaching out into the shallows; I made out several dim figures standing by a narwhal – one of them was the elderly man with the red beard. Beside him, two policemen were unrolling a rope which they then fixed to pickets planted in the sand. It was only then that I saw Burke, awkwardly sprawled over the narwhal, knees bent, arms thrown out; its tusk had skewered his stomach, to reappear, reddened with blood, between his shoulder blades. His expression was one of amazement, even slight amusement; or perhaps incredulous, amazed to have met such a death.

'Do you know this man?' the inspector asked me curtly.

'Yes, he's called Klaus Burke; he's my travelling companion,' I answered faintly. The inspector held out his arms, as though to apologise.

'We can't understand how this could have happened! There are no witnesses. It must have been at about one o'clock; the mist had already cleared, and the tide was beginning to turn. Perhaps the creature was trying to ease itself off the sea bed, and felt threatened,' he suggested in some agitation.

The man with the red beard now joined us, shaking his head.

'That's not possible. This morning that one was already dead!' he objected. Then, turning to me, he added:

'When we met. Remember?'

He waded a few steps into the water towards the creature, then bent down to run his hand over its pectoral fin.

'Anyway, a beached narwhal can't use its tusk; it's a physiological impossibility!' he shouted, lifting his nose and thrusting his hips forwards in imitation of a narwhal's slithering gait. The inspector put his hands into his pockets and looked at him severely.

'Take him away!' he said to the policemen, who were

standing some distance away, holding a stretcher.

I glanced with some distaste at Burke's crumpled body as they lifted it clear of the tusk; meeting his glassy stare, I thought perhaps he had met the death that he desired.

I returned to the hotel in some bewilderment. The foyer was deserted; the waiters were picking up the dirty glasses and emptying the ashtrays. I went up to my room and stretched out on the bed, trying to sleep; but I lay awake, tossing and turning, until it was very late. Sensing I had a fever, I wrapped myself up in all the covers I could find and then at last I did sleep a bit, though very uneasily. I was sweating, but my flesh had come out in goose-pimples from the cold. I was woken by the sound of rain on the roof; day was breaking, my fever seemed to have abated and my forehead felt unexpectedly cool, though I still felt weak. I threw off the drenched covers and went over to the window: the sea was grey and foam-flecked, fanning out over the beach in broad frothy waves. The cruise ship was still there, lights ablaze, funnels smoking; it hooted twice, as though preparing to depart. I was desperately thirsty; I took a long drink of water from the tap, then took off my clothes and had a wash, noting that my reflection in the mirror was yellower and more stooped then ever. There were yellowish marks around my eyes; my teeth were chattering, though whether from cold or fear I wasn't sure. I went down to the restaurant, downed a coffee and went out for a listless walk along the beach, my head thronged with a ragbag of thoughts I couldn't piece together. Memories of my year-long wanderings were paraded before me like snaps in a photo album, the last one being the awful lifeless mask that was Burke's face. The streets were empty; a few coloured umbrellas were opening up on the landing-stages near the aquarium. I wandered back to the hotel without the faintest idea of what I was going to do.

After Klaipeda, the only place left on the list was Tallinn: the last stage of my journey, the dead end of the maze in which I was lost. I was trying to escape the maelstrom for which I was headed, but I knew there was no way out. I thought back to the mysterious house on Perkelos Gatve, and a shudder ran down my spine; perhaps Burke had been murdered, and his murderer was now hot on my trail. I looked around me at the houses, the blocks of flats, the unlit windows, and imagined a gun pointing in my direction, an eye patiently seeking me out in the cross hairs. No, my death was never going to be that easy; the diabolical captain of my fate would never have been satisfied with so little. Almost reassured, I went back to the hotel with the intention of trying to get some sleep before making a decision. I told the man at the reception desk that I was leaving; I didn't want to admit as much to myself, but I knew I would be going on to Tallinn. I paid the bill and went up to my room; as I pushed the door open, I saw something on the floor. It was a picture postcard of Klaipeda; on the back, in spidery, nervous writing, was one word: *Toompea*.

I pushed the door closed with my foot and paced up and down the room, scrutinising the postcard down to the last detail: it was a view of the harbour, the very same one I could see from my own window. I peered out through the rain-streaked glass: the bay, the aquarium, the landing-stages, the seafront. All that was missing on the postcard was the ship. Smoke was now pouring from both funnels and I could make out the dim outlines of the queue of cars driving up the gangway and into the hold, their headlights reflected in the puddles. Suddenly the sun burst through the clouds and the coppery sunlight lit up the side of the ship. *Toompea*, I read on its riveted sheet metal, and at that moment the hooter sounded again, as though it were hailing my discovery. I rushed downstairs without even bothering to take my luggage.

'The ship!' I shouted in the direction of the porter, making him jump.

'The *Toompea*, when does she leave?'

'This morning,'

'And where's she headed for?'

'Tallinn!'

I hurtled towards the quay at breakneck speed, dashing across the road between the honking cars and through the passenger terminal until at last I found myself beside the ship. The anchor chain was being weighed with a deafening clang, the ropes were being lifted from the moorings, but the gangway was still open. The sailor on duty didn't play hard to get: he pocketed the wad of dollars I offered him, and a few minutes later I was on deck, puffing and panting, watching Klaipeda receding into the distance and finally disappearing altogether, eclipsed by the grey furrows of the sea.

I stayed holed up in my cabin until late in the afternoon; only when I saw the light fading through the porthole did I dare venture up on deck. The sailor had brought me a travel document stating that I had embarked at Kiel; he had taken down my passport details, and also demanded another few hundred dollars, since he had to square it with the man in the ticket-office in order that everything should appear in order. I sat down in the bar on the lower deck, which was quieter than the others. I was hungry, but didn't dare go to the restaurant; I was afraid that whoever had lured me on board the *Toompea* might be setting me a trap. I was hoping somehow to recognise my mysterious pursuer before he noticed me. I peered through the glass into the neighbouring restaurant, scrutinising every face, even those of the waiters, while bolting down peanuts to take the edge off my hunger. That night I barricaded myself in my cabin, and set the alarm clock to wake me every hour, at which point I would check the door and even the screws on the porthole.

The following morning, the sea was calm and bright. It was a peerless June day, white foam was dancing on the tips of the green waves at the ship's side; people leant over the handrails, lifting their faces to the warm, light wind. Children were playing, elderly couples were having their photographs taken on the sun-drenched decks; there was a party mood afoot. I too wanted to join that carefree crowd, and went to sit on a bench on the lower deck, out of the wind, from which there was a view of a distant coastline: possibly Latvia, I thought.

In the afternoon the light changed, the blue of the sea became more intense and a strong wind got up. The crowd on deck thinned out and most people drifted off inside; through the glass I could see small family groups seated in front of cups of steaming chocolate. Only a few couples were now left in the deckchairs. I too went inside. Wandering around along the upper decks, I found myself in the corridors outside the first-class cabins; I checked the swimmers jumping off the diving boards in the swimming-pool, ambled around among the fruit machines in the casino, where elderly ladies, their handbags clutched close to their chests, were stubbornly sending coloured images whirring in the hopes of seeing a flood of coins suddenly pouring out of the chrome funnels. But I had absolutely no pointer as to which of these unknown faces might be that of the man who had drawn me aboard the *Toompea* and, without such knowledge, I might be walking straight into the fatal trap which would be my undoing. I couldn't imagine what form my death would take – whether I too would be transfixed by a narwhal's tusk, charred to a cinder in the boilers in the engine-room or drowned at sea, my body mauled by the propellers. At all events, I'd had enough of waiting, so I resigned myself to the idea of revealing myself; that was the only way to make something happen. I went into the restaurant and sat down at a table in the middle; I ate my meal slowly, peering round me in search of a face, a glance. I chose fine wines and complicated dishes, requiring the attentions of several waiters; to prolong my stay, I also ordered coffee, liqueurs and cigars. Smoke and alcohol caused my mind to glaze over; I was so tired that I could hardly see. But I carried on studying the room, staring so blatantly at my fellow-diners that I alarmed the ladies and puzzled the men in their blue suits. Finally, hoisting myself wearily out of my seat, I decided to go out on deck again, choosing a sunny spot in the bows, where the wind was at its strongest, and the waters were severed majestically by the prow of the great ship as it made its way eastwards. On the deck below me a sailor was rolling up some ropes; seagulls were hovering patiently in search of food. People were starting to come out again; children were playing, women were sunbathing in deckchairs, their eyes screwed up against the sun.

Suddenly a girl ran towards the handrail, shouting as she did so. The sailor dropped his rope and looked out to sea, shielding his eyes with his hand. I too got up to cast a look over the expanse of glittering water: some distance from the ship, in a strip of sea that looked calmer than the rest, I saw a shoal of narwhals darting in and out of the darker water, their long tusks glittering fiercely, like a barrier of gigantic thorns slung over the sea; they were ducking, then re-emerging, perfectly aligned. I noticed another shoal, nearer the horizon, swimming slowly in serried ranks, their tusks all pointed in the same direction, as though engaged in some mass migration, their backs glinting in the late afternoon sunlight. Some were lighter in colour, almost white; others were black, with leathery, lumpy noses.

At that moment the hooter sounded, and the ship slowed down and began to roll; the loudspeakers gave out the alarm signal and the red lights in front of the doors leading to the cabins began to flash. Sailors rushed out on deck and began loosening the ropes of a lifeboat. I stood aside to get out of their way and went to join a group of people leaning against the railings; it was then that I realised that I was the only person looking at the narwhals. The crowd around me were pointing at something in the other direction; I screwed up my eyes and looked out to sea in the direction of their pointing fingers.

'Man overboard!' a sailor shouted.

Amidst the glare, some ten metres from the ship, I caught sight of something floating – something that looked distinctly sinister. Life jackets were thrown out and the lifeboat was lowered into the water. All eyes were on the blurred shape bobbing on the surface. Sailors with harpoons climbed down into the boat but soon started shaking their heads and waving their oars in the direction of the ship. The dripping lifeboat was hauled up again, and a hideously bloated body was laid out on the deck amidst a now silent crowd. Two nurses with a resuscitator appeared and applied it to the man's chest; his body quivered, his arms twitched and his knees shook, but the nurses exchanged gloomy glances. After a couple more attempts they put their resuscitator back in its case. They were about to cover him with plastic sheeting when I pushed my way forward through the silent crowd and stared in horror at the corpse:

'I know that man!'

Seized with a sudden fit of dizziness, I almost fell; a sailor caught me and sat me down on a nearby bench. Someone undid my shirt and gave me some smelling salts.

'Barnung's his name, Herbert Barnung,' I murmured, before passing out.

When I came to, I found myself in a first-aid post in Tallinn harbour; a worried-looking doctor was taking my blood pressure. He shook his head and said something to a nurse seated at the other side of my camp-bed.

'The doctor is asking whether you suffer from any illnesses,' she said stiffly in German. With some difficulty, I sat up.

'No, absolutely not. I have to go now!' I said, in something of a panic. The less time I spent here, the better, it seemed to me.

The doctor talked on, this time at length. Looking gravely first at me, then at the nurse, he shook the thermometer and pointed his finger at his blood pressure machine. The nurse just looked at me sadly; all she said was:

'The doctor says you're very ill!'

I got down from the camp-bed and picked up my clothes from the chair. The doctor unbuttoned his gown and left the room. The nurse put up a screen and sat waiting for me seated at a small green desk.

'Where is Dr. Barnung?' I asked brusquely.

The nurse shook her head and looked at me expectantly.

'The drowned man! The one they fished up from the sea!'

Then the nurse nodded, stood up and took me into the next room, where I found the sailor who had come to my aid, together with an officer from the harbour office.

'How are you feeling?'

'Better, thank you.'

'All in a day's work. A drowned man is never a pretty

sight!' he added, perhaps hoping to make me feel better, then went on:

'So, you knew this man?'

'I did. His name is Herbert Barnung. He's a neurologist – a German citizen, from Munich,' I replied with bitter certainty.

The sailor and the man from the harbour office exchanged puzzled looks; passing a plastic package one to the other, they briefly conferred. It was the nurse who spoke next; she took a passport out of the package and handed it to me.

'There must be some mistake, sir. This is the passport we found in his pocket.'

I opened the sodden document and leafed through it. Under Dr. Barnung's photograph I saw the words: Mirko Stolojan, born Kaliningrad 28 August 1946, which caused me promptly to sit down in the chair again and run my hand over my forehead; seeing me do so, the nurse offered me a glass of water, which I downed in a single swallow, then sat there staring at the two men. The sailor scratched his nose, then gazed into space; the man from the harbour office put the passport back in the folder and shrugged.

'All in a day's work. A drowned man is never a pretty sight!' he said again with an embarrassed smile.

It was only the beginning of August, but Tallinn had the air of a city whose tourist season was drawing to a close. The bus I'd taken from the harbour drove through the outskirts, then into a residential area with a lot of greenery, on the west side of the bay. In the distance I could see the outlines of low, sandy islands, covered with shrubs. The ferries lined up in the harbour were all empty, their gangways cordoned off; on board, a few listless hostesses were sitting around chatting at a table on the empty deck. A quiet sea lay under a clear, cold sky; small waves were lapping against the quay. The low afternoon light was falling on the trunks of the silver birches, and the woods seemed alight with an eerie glow. Beyond the wooden landing-stages, amidst sandbanks dotted with thorny plants, a fragile canebrake was bowing silently, ruffled by a light wind blowing from the moss-strewn shore. Seated on the harbour wall, an old man was fishing, the line he held wound around his fingers catching the light like a thread of cobweb underneath a pine tree.

On the quay, amidst the orderly tubs of geraniums, an ice-cream seller was polishing the brass fittings of his cart; then he put down his cloth, leant over the lid and rubbed out strawberry and chocolate from the list of flavours written on the glass. All he had now was vanilla. It was a windy Sunday afternoon, scented with sugar and shoe polish. The sound of a barrel organ wafted in fitfully from the funfair on the narrow strip of pinewood that closed in the bay. My eye was caught by the mirrors of a roundabout glinting in the sun, and I decided to follow the crowd attracted by such merriment.

At the entrance, a cluster of coloured balloons were swaying around in the wind; a child grabbed at the balloon-seller's wrist and pulled on the string of one of them, looking beseechingly towards his mother. A girl was handing out blue paper flags; now every family was sporting one, slipped into their caps, attached to their rucksacks or fixed to a pushchair. I followed the crowd of jostling children, who were constantly tripping each other up as they paused to pull up their sagging socks, jumping around and dropping sweets from their bursting pockets. Once inside, I was enclasped in a damp warmth; there was a smell of chlorine and sodden wood. The uproar from the floor below rose and fell in volume as though those who were making it were cheering on the runners of some unseen race. Up here, people were scurrying between two barriers, moving in the direction of the ticket-office. I stared blankly at the writing above the various windows, noticed a green light flashing on and off. I proffered a banknote to the woman at the till and took my ticket, allowing myself to be jostled by the crowd in the direction of a blue glass door. Such was the crush that I couldn't see anything directly in front of me, but beyond the door, which led into a large circular room surrounded by banked-up steps like a stadium, I could see the glimmer of water reflected on the ceiling; I realised that I had ended up in a covered swimming-pool, where some competition was being held, and I was just about to turn tail in disappointment when my attention was caught by a board with coloured writing on it. As I gazed uncomprehendingly at the odd letters of that unknown language, I had the sudden feeling that in fact they contained something that was known to me. I stepped forward for a better view and read, in fine Gothic letters:

Vancouver
San Diego
Papeete
Vladivostok
Pusan
Taipei
Surabaya
Durban
Eilat
Constanta
Odessa
Klaipeda
Tallinn

Elbowing shocked mothers out of my path, and being roundly insulted in return as they tried to shield their delicate offspring from my violent advance, I now turned round and carried on with my attempt to approach the pool; I received rabbit punches, someone grabbed me by the scruff of my neck, but my devilishly sharp elbows got the better of them. I stumbled, and got back on my feet; dragging myself along the wall, I found myself at last beside the pool.

And there he was, standing on a dais in the middle of it; waiting until everyone had fallen absolutely silent, he slowly raised his arms, threw back his head and uttered a long whistling sound, almost a howl, which rang out in the air for a few moments, setting my eardrums pulsing, then subsided into a quieter gurgling sound, only to rise again into a cheerful twitter. At that same moment, four dolphins leapt out of the water and swam towards him, flapping their flat tails; raising their snouts, their mouths half-open as though they were laughing, they answered him with that same whistle. The interpreter lowered his arms again, and the gurgling became a deep growl; the dolphins fell silent and sank back into the water, propelling themselves off to the four corners of the pool with quick flicks of the tail, their dorsal fins flashing along the surface of the water, then executing a quick tour of the water before once more arranging themselves around the dais, raising themselves on their tails. Encircling the interpreter in their hypnotic dance, they opened and shut their mouths, waving their pectoral fins and shaking their sides, their eyes on the now silent man. Motionless, chin lowered, he himself was beginning to look like one of them: his chest seemed marked by the same yellowish, keel-like ridges as their own, his calves were puckered with the same grey stalk-like structures as those which swelled out at the base of their caudal fins. Almost as one, the four creatures emitted a low, moaning sound, then slid silently to the bottom of the pool; the interpreter raised his arms again, puffed out his hairless chest and let out four different-sounding whistles, jerking his head in each of the four directions as he did so. He was staring into the middle distance, his mouth pursed and his neck as swollen as that of a snake about to strike, stretching out his fingers and lifting his elbows slightly, as though about to take flight. The people on the stands were gazing at him in silent amazement. I sniffed the air, awaiting the usual bitter stench, which did indeed soon envelop me; strangely, though, I noted that it was no longer one of wood and resin, but rather of brackish seaweed, of the insides of dead shells, of the cold depths of the ocean; the smell of the narwhals from Klaipeda, of the yellow mud inside the wreck in Odessa. After a few moments, one by one the dorsal fins reappeared on the surface, and the creatures again started leaping up in front of the dais, their movements perfectly in time with the interpreter's whistles. They dived down again, and after swimming around for a while they lined up on one side of the pool, turning their impenetrable black eyes towards the stands. Heedless of the frantic applause, the interpreter was still staring into space with a haunted expression on his face, arching his shoulders and moving his mouth as though it were a beak. It was then that he caught sight of me, clinging to a railing, paralysed by fear. He leant forwards on the dais and waved his fist in my direction, shouting out triumphantly:

'So there you are! Did you hear it? I told you it existed! The primordial aquatic language once spoken by us all, and still concealed in each of our imperfect earthly tongues! The language of when we were fish, dark scaly inhabitants of the ocean's depths, and God didn't even know he had created us. I told you so! Well, I've discovered it! I speak it! I am the only man in the world who can talk to dolphins!'

I collapsed on to the wet tiles and wept furiously, as I had never wept before.

I've lived in the Tallinn Aquarium for years now; it's one of just sixteen in the world which have a dolphinarium, as do Constanta, Odessa and Klaipeda.

I look after the dolphins. Kim, Kaina, Leda and Ferdinand are young striated dolphins originally from the Atlantic, and one of the more vocal species, together with the common dolphin. They are the only ones whose whistles can be heard on the surface, even if made deep under the water. Each morning I bring them four kilos of krill and, in the evening, live whitefish; in the spring I also give them herrings and freshwater crayfish which we get from the nearby canning factory.

The symptoms produced by Dr. Barnung's lethal therapy are gradually abating, though every so often I still get my languages mixed up, particularly at a change of season. My attacks last for several hours, like a fever, causing me to utter sounds I can't control, and at such times – because, for no reason, I feel ashamed of them – I go and take refuge in the aquarium. Although the line between madness and normality no longer seems so clear to me, I continue to feel that my animal whistling is somehow aberrant; at such moments the dolphins put their heads out of the pool and listen to me curiously; they point their snouts in the air and wave them around as though they were trying to smell something. Then they lay their heads on the dais and stare at me, as puzzled as I myself, and somehow disappointed.

According to the interpreter, they cannot understand me; it

seems that I speak the rare language of the southern Tursiops, which are shy and solitary, and live in the Sea of Japan and round the Kuril Islands.

Over time, reflecting on such little information as I managed to extract from my silent companion, I gleaned that Stauber and Dr. Barnung were in cahoots to rob him of his secret and boast of being the first to understand the primordial language of dolphins. What I had not known was that, in the past, Dr. Barnung had worked as an interpreter for the Soviet Politburo, under the name of Mirko Stolojan. I read as much in an old newspaper cutting I found when I was poking around among his possessions. He had then become the director of a psychiatric clinic in Nahodka, in the Sea of Japan; the photo showed him wearing the uniform of a medical officer, and a moustache. Apparently he'd been doing experiments with cetaceans, recording their whistling sounds and playing them round the clock in the patients' rooms. People who were there at the time say that the most serious schizophrenics started imitating them. But then the clinic closed for lack of funds.

Dr. Barnung fled to the West and took on a false identity. The whistling men began to wander all over Russia, instinctively looking for the sea, where they would be able to hear the dolphins' call. Dr. Barnung continued his experiments in Munich – on patients in the linguistic clinic where I too ended up. He'd secretly incorporated the cetaceans' whistles into the tapes with which he'd constantly bombard us; so, without realising it, we'd learned them. They bored into our minds, wormed themselves into us from within. What Dr. Barnung didn't realise was that he was inoculating us with the rare language of the southern Tursiops, which is almost unknown in the ocean depths, and that may explain why his experiment failed. Like us, the various kinds of cetaceans have difficulty in understanding one other, and the ocean depths are peopled by creatures with no descendants, the last of a race that is dying but not yet extinct, and which cry out, unheeded, in their solitude. So I am even more alone: excluded even from the watery world into which I was unnaturally thrust, I talk a language which is a mental illness.

It was undoubtedly Dr. Barnung who murdered Stauber in Odessa, and hurled the unsuspecting Burke on to the tusk of the dead narwhal on the beach in Klaipeda. I too was on his list. He had not managed to rid himself of me with his therapies, so he had lured me on to the *Toompea*. But he himself had ended up drowned in his own pursuit of the narwhals.

So what had once struck me as a series of machinations now appears something else entirely. It would seem that chance alone brought me here: the ravings of a lunatic, whose path quite simply happened to cross my own, and nothing more; the experiments of a criminal neurologist, and the jealousy of a head of department for one of his subordinates had done the rest. It could have happened to anyone, and it happened to me – though it is undeniable that I was exposing myself to risk by mixing with insane deviants such as interpreters, people with slippery, unformed identities, in whose company sprinklings of the irrational are more likely to insinuate themselves and further crook humanity's already crooked timber. Only among their like could a man be mad enough to want to talk with dolphins, confusing human with animal and imitating everything he hears and sees, from the rustling of leaves to the soughing of wind, from the glassy-eyed stare of a fish to the heat haze hanging over a desert. Even now that I see him every day, I can never remember what he looked like a moment ago, I cannot fix him in my memory. Each time I look at him, it's as though I'm seeing something different: as different, indeed, as a landscape from a tree, or a stretch of sky, or one of his dolphins. He's not a human being, he has no soul, no personality; he is a remnant, something left over from the cosmic slime when it was nothing and could have become anything. I alone among men have seen through him into the gulf from which the world emerged; I alone bear witness, and I cannot share my knowledge with any other living soul.

Today I am known as Tibor Preda, and this name – not my own – is the only one I can still bear. For I am the fruit of a mistake, a monstrous creature which should have died of the poisonous inoculations to which it was subjected. Yet I survived, and the man who engaged in such ruthless tinkering with fate seems to have cast me from his mind; abandoning his researches in mid-stream, he has condemned me to an existence lived out in a state of suspended animation, a victim of unremitting torment. But sometimes it occurs to me that there might be another, hidden meaning to this anguish, something I shall understand only with time. Perhaps the experiment for which I served as guinea pig is still under way, and this is just a phase, a stage in the metamorphosis I'm undergoing. I'm living in a bell jar, surrounded by particles of unknown substances which are splitting and cohering as in alchemy, able to transform all humanity into cetaceans over the course of a few generations.

At times I thought of going home; of ending my days in a psychiatric clinic, together with my secret. After all, time has passed, and perhaps no one now remembers the Beast of Bukovina. But I am bound to this man by a force which is irresistible; if I strayed from his side, I feel that I'd be lost,

215

sucked into a maelstrom of pain; and utterly, unbearably alone. Still unsure when my time will come, I lack the courage to expose myself to further suffering. Here, at least the days slip by without incident, without my coming to any harm. So far, the vice which was destined to crush me has bitten in vain. I have learned Estonian, and I show parties of school-children and tourists around the dolphinarium; I've been given a green uniform and a cap with a plastic peak with a label saying 'Interpreter'. Although it was never my intention, I have become one of them; children regard me with awe, mothers give me tips. On Sundays I help the interpreter with the 'singing' sessions; I hand him the hoops through which he makes the dolphins jump, and the balls that they balance on their snouts. And when I hear their whistling, their lowing, those sounds which, once alarming, have now become so familiar to me; when I see them rising from the water beside their trainer, shaking their heads with that enigmatic smile of theirs, I wonder whether they too, like me, might not be slaves to this man, prisoners of his contagious madness.

Sometimes I even feel homesick for Dr. Barnung's clinic and its iron discipline; I realise with amazement that the months spent in that sunny laboratory repeating exercises in Romanian may have been the happiest of my life. Perhaps there was method in his madness; perhaps all that Romanian really did do me good. Somehow, that light, lilting language made my inner rift easier to bear, went some way towards healing the wound I feel throbbing within me in my long hours of solitude – unlike Estonian, which is a stealthy, thorny language, full of barbs, sinking itself into the mind like a fish-hook and never letting go.

Quite recently, I have begun to pray; I creep into church of a morning and kneel down with the unbeliever's mild sense of

216

guilt. All I am asking is to understand: if I am being punished, all I ask is to know why. If I am but a trifle batted to and fro by the talons of fate, I ask God for a sign. If he truly is omnipotent, I ask him to free me of this punishment, or to have done with me once and for all. If he can do nothing for me, I ask him to enable me to abandon hope. But, looking at the crucifix on the altar, there in the silence of that lonely little wooden church, I am suddenly struck by the awful feeling that it is I who am a mistake, that all humanity is just an accident; that God himself is a dolphin, up there in his heaven, whistling mockingly at my prayers, flapping his fins and waving his snout in the celestial heights of a watery paradise.